A

SCHEME

IN EVERY

SCENE

Hzal Anubewei Fudge

A SCHEME IN EVERY SCENE © 2015 by Hzal Anubewei Fudge.

Book and Cover design by Oetryhouse

ISBN 978-1-7346413-0-1
Library of Congress: TXu000647850

Second Edition: February 2020

Hzal Anubewei Fudge
PO BOX 217
STONE MTN, GA 30086
hzalfa2003@gmail.com

Dedicated to my Dad, William Fudge Sr.,
one of the greatest story tellers ever!

TABLE OF CONTENTS

...where the wind sits...

BETHOSE

They

never felt the lurking in the wind that brought him. Not that the wind had a body but old Gwynda believed in the signs of the wind. Yet, the man had slipped past them all.

Viona

was one of those sweet females. She had just reached the age of ripeness when the man appeared. Her fields were full of juice.

Viona

came upon him one day in the lemon orchard.

-what you doing in the lemons?

-eating them-

-who told you to eat them lemons?

-you did-

Viona

walked into the lemon field where the man was sitting under the biggest lemon tree in the field. Lemon peels covered the ground.

-you done ate a whole bushel of lemons. what's wrong with you, you crazy or something?

-nothing wrong with me. I love lemons. I was in Florida when I heard about your lemons. A man name Brown something or other told me about your lemons so I came to see-

-you mean you walked all the way from Florida up here just to taste my lemons?

-sure did and that Mr. Brown was right. Yo Mississippi Bottom Lemons is the best I ever had and I've eaten lemons all over the South-

Gwynda

said something was odd about that man. Said he

walked between the winds.

The

man picked himself up and walked out of the lemon field back to the road. Viona picked up her legs and followed after the man.

-where you going? I don't even know your name-

-my name is Tan and I'm going back to Florida, I think or maybe I'll just go north-

-well, Tan don't you think you need to rest some before you go?

-rest where?

Viona

felt trapped. She couldn't explain the emotion that grabbed her but she couldn't let this man that had walked so far to taste her lemons just walk out of her life without knowing more about him. That's how Viona lost her heart for the lemon man.

The

lost man was Hickson. He had loved Viona since

they were kids. His grandfather raised chickens, hogs and in his long fields he kept corn and peas and had the best pecan trees in the county. Granny kept her own garden she picked from daily. She planted tomatoes, potatoes, radishes, onions, lettuce, celery, and beets. Hickson's daddy started the soybean and peanut fields and had the best watermelon patch this side of the moon. That was where Hickson and Viona found themselves every summer busting the sweetest watermelons, eating and laughing until darkness and the mosquitoes chased them from the fields.

Now

that Viona was with Tan, Hickson was the lost man. He had no taste for the watermelons growing in his father's fields.

Viona

felt the eyes of Hickson fall down on her shoulders where his arms used to be. Tan raised his own eyes when the three of them came together in front of Ms. Gwynda' s house store.

-Hello Hickson, I'm glad I ran into you. I want you to meet....

-Know all about it already. Got me a busy day. I'll talk to you later-

Gwynda was watching from the side door where she sold little sweets and stuff. She saw the wind was just lurking around, not moving, just waiting. As soon as Tan moved the wind rushed in around Viona as if trying to save her.

-Gwynda I wonder if you would taste this-

It was a jug of lemonade.

-What for?

-Well, I was thinking of selling it, Tan says my lemons are the best in the South-

-Who made it, him?

The tip of her two fingers pointed at the lemon man.

-Well no, yes . . . I mean we both did-

-Don't wanna taste it-

Gwynda

had never turned her back on nobody. It was a terrible thing to do. This unhappiness jumped on the back of the wind of ill repute and spread itself evenly throughout the whole county.

Sadness

hung around Viona because the wind stayed away from Tan. Nobody wanted her lemonade and if they had tasted it they would have known how sweet and delicious it was.

The

next thing that happened really shocked all that knew Viona. She told Hickson that she was leaving.

-But where will you go Viona?

-Well, Tan said since won't nobody here taste my lemonade this place ain't fit for us no more. It's Gwynda's fault. All that talk about the wind. Why, she act like Tan is evil or something? He likes my lemons. Some people like sour things-

-not by the bushel full Viona. I seen him the other day chewing like a machine. It wasn't natural.

Viona

wouldn't listen and in a few days she was leaving with the lemon man Tan. She looked at her lemon orchard and saw that one of the trees had withered and died. On others the leaves had turned brown.

-need more rain-

Tan said matter-of-factly chewing on one of the two lemons he had just picked.

-everything will be fine once we get to New York-

-New York? but I thought we was going to Florida. what we gone do with all these seeds in New York. Lemons won't grow there it's too cold. Besides I don't like cities, I ain't got no room for my mind there-

-you'll be ok.-

Tan never stopped walking as they headed for the train. Nobody waved goodbye as they left and for the first time Viona shed a tear. She realized at that moment she had never cried. In fact she just realized that she had never seen anybody cry.

Gwynda

watched Viona leaving and saw the wind part as the train left the station. The town of Bethose in the county of Bethose lost one of its own. Hickson sat in the watermelon field with tears in his eyes so sad that the wind couldn't dry them. It was a sad day.

The

cold bit Viona's hands and feet. Tan was out again in search of lemons. The first year went well and the lemonade made from the fields of Viona was the best anyone in New York had ever tasted. Viona needed to get back before winter to prune the field. Tan argued with her and closed the door. He did the same in the spring and sent men who did not know the fields to tend to them. They came back with the news of withered trees and dry seasons and weak soil and mosquitos swarming from an untended watermelon patch nearby. Hickson had taken to drinking and swearing and fighting.

Viona

fell into a state of despondence. Tan argued more now. He ordered lemons from Florida and mixed them with the lemons from Viona's orchard. The whole batch withered and the lemon business fell under. Viona sold the last three one hundred bags of sugar to a Pakistani. Tan was becoming more irritable now that he had no lemons to eat and would be gone for hours searching. Five years came and went so fast Viona couldn't believe time traveled that fast. The city closed in on her and its many winds blew hard jumping off the buildings or the clouds hurrying by. The winter wind was the worst as it sent debris flying through the air. Tan never complained about the wind. It seemed to avoid him as he walked. She thought it was her imagination but the more she watched she saw what the wind did. Viona now saw that the face of Tan had changed. She regretted now having ever left Bethose and her field of lemons. The thousands of dollars they had made the first two years was nearly gone. The only thing Tan worked was his appetite for lemons. Viona still made lemonade but New York had turned against its flavor and only newcomers filled with old rumors came for the once famous Mississippi Bottom Lemonade.

One

day in March when the wind was really blowing hard and knocking things around she was looking out the window and she saw this tall shadow moving between the wind and even the children who were playing saw it and were pointing. Viona's heart skittered as she recognized the man inside the walking shadow flowing between the winds. Anger flowed around the figure like torrential rain. That was the day Tan brought thunder into the house shattering what remained of Viona's innocence forever.

-there are no lemons here, none. I have looked everywhere and I can't find one. something has happened to the lemons. some man at the market said the seeds got mixed up from different parts of the country and trees are withering away.

something is killing the damn lemon trees. why are you looking at me like that. it's not my fault I... I love lemons, the way they taste. I could eat a whole bushel, maybe two. why are you staring at me like that. your eyes look like brown lemons. I aint no ghost I'm just hungry. go out and find me some lemons, hurry-

Viona

traveled all day on the train and found two lemons. Tan was now looking withered and drawn up. He greedily ate the two lemons whole.

-more, more. Viona you know I got to have them, help me please-

The

eyes of Tan came into the world of pity. He was in no shape to care for himself as moment by moment he deteriorated into a deep listless existence. Viona scoured the city every day but the situation only grew worse. They had little money left and she was becoming ill herself.

Then

one morning she woke up to find him gone. He had taken the ring he had bought her, probably to pawn it she thought. She waited five days for him to return. It was the middle of April when she headed home.

Gwynda

woke up early and saw a bright wind coming from the north. The wind was sailing, whipping through the town as if it were dancing. The last time she had seen that was when grandpa Hickson died and they had a great going home celebration. Yet, the wind of sadness that usually announces such occasions was nowhere to be found. So Gwynda decided to take a sit and wait. It wasn't long before the train came and the wind became more excited. Gwynda got to her feet. Hickson had come in town. A week ago for no reason at all he had stopped drinking and returned to his fields promising this would be the best season of watermelons he had ever grown.

Viona

stepped from the train back on the soil of Bethose making herself happy for the first time in years. She was older and wiser. Gwynda and Hickson greeted her warmly. A celebration was held that night and the wind moved among the participants with warmth, even keeping away some of the more pesky mosquitos.

Everything was back to normal now that Viona was home and she brought wisdom with her and talked more openly when she wasn't in her lemon orchard.

Nobody ever heard what had become of Tan the lemon man but Gwynda kept her eye open now for any person or thing that could walk between the wind.

... they thought they had closed their eyes...

PROMISES KEPT

The

moon set so low on the side of the hill it looked like a big eye peeking through the window. It was a red eye.

-they got Pete and Troy and Box and two other boys I didn't know-

—slow down boy, running in here like the devil himself on your tail. now who got Pete and Troy?

-the white folks got'um-

-got'um where?

-down by the big tree, across the river-

-Pete and Troy know better than to go on that side of the river, aint nothing over there but white trash. decent white folks don't go nowhere near that place-

-well, they was over with that white boy, Johnny and some white girl they call Nan-

-Cisco what we gone do?

-how many white folks was over there, Paul?

-I don't know, a whole lot maybe a hundred. they was making so much noise. they was drinking and they had Pete and nem tied up-

-what about the white boy, was he tied up too?

-yup, they had roped him to a wheel on a wagon

-the white girl, was she there?

-there was two white girls on the ground on they faces and they wasn't moving or nothing

I heard somebody say they was dead-

-Millie what you me want me to do. they got my boys over there, surrounded by them white folks. they got they hands on'm. what you want me to do?

I don't guess there's a whole lot we can do. the white folks got they hands on them, same as they did my daddy's brother ten years ago. got him down by the tree and hung him. had a picnic while they burned his body-

-----

-Johnny you sure about this. that old man almost caught us the last time we got in his still-

-Troy quit worrying. that's why I brought Nan along to distract that old coot while we get the liquor. all we got to do is get about two hundred bottles, get over to Mississippi. I got a cousin over there that said he'll buy all we bring. the feds busted up the ones in his area. he said they need some of that shine as quick as possible—

-yeah but how Nan gone get close to that old' man he don't trust nobody-

-you boys worry too much Pete. Nan knows his daughter Maybelle. she told Nan how the old man gets drunk every Friday and then that horny bastard comes after her-

-his own daughter?

-that ain't none of his daughter. Pete you remember that woman that Sanchez brought up from Texas when we was kids? Well, anyway she died and that's her kid. the old man took her in and been having his way with her ever since. she told Nan all about it so her and Nan became friends. one Friday the old man got drunk and tried to come after Nan but she got away-

-O, so you figure he'll try again tonight-

-yeah, but I told Nan make sure to get that old' coot good and liquored up-

-what about the other girl, Maybelline?

-her name's Maybelle. she said she'd help us if I took her to Mississippi-

-I don't know if that's such a good idea. two white

women traveling in a truck with us at night-

-Nan can sit up front with me while I drive and Maybelle can sit in the back with yaw-

-you gone put one woman in the back with four of us-

-she's more Spanish than white-

-alright Nan you know what you got to do. remember one thing don't drink too much of that shine that's strong stuff-

-don't worry me *granpappy* had a still when I was growing up. I've had my share of liquor and horny uncles. I know how to handle this. besides me and Maybelle planned something special for that old coot that will get his attention for sure. you just get out to that still where I told you Maybelle said he had moved it-

-----

-so yaw done come back. old Mr. Double got something for ya gal-

-heard you got the best shine this side of

Arkansas so I thought I come by to taste it-

-gal I got the best shine in three states. ain't that right Nan-

-everybody knows you got the best shine around-

-what's that you wearing Maybelle? we got company, why you dressed like that?

-she's a woman just like me. got the same things I do. do you mind me like this Nan?

-no, I likes it fine. I think I'd like it better though if old Mr. Double gave me some of that shine of his-

-sho, sho... you girls acting like you horny or something-

-stop talking so much old man and get that shine out-

-hurry up get that stuff loaded-

-we's moving as fast as we can-

-Johnny how much you think we gone git on this-

-two dollars a bottle boys-

-how much is that-

-Pete where you get these boys. yaw don't know how to count, that's two hundred dollars-

-what you say-

-Troy hush up, we ain't got time for all this talking, let's hurry and get finished. we been up here almost a hour. we got to get back down the hill and get Nan and Maybelle and get the hell out of here-

-who you boys? uh uh put your hands where I can see'um. 'preciate you boys loading up that truck for us. been watching you for the last twenty minutes. tonight, is our pickup night. oh, you didn't know about that? yeah, same time every Friday.

-that's right put those last few bottles on there. hey, Roy look at this here boy, shaking like a leaf. you don't reckon it's this little old shotgun pointing at his black head do you-

-naw Nathan. you want a drink boy to calm your nerves-

-now what you girls got planned for old Double-

-well, we thought you might like your own private dance show. turn on that radio Maybelle. you like dance girls don't you Mr. Double-

-sho I do. Maybelle get me that special shine out of that cupboard over there. on the second shelf behind the sugar-

-here you go dahlin child, now taste this. one hundred proof of the smoothest shine around. I kept some of these for myself it was so good. yaw drink some of this-

-damn Mr. Double that is good shine. Here Maybelle drink some of this. hoo wee I feel like dancing-

-let me get a swig of that. you gals is kinda greedy ain't you. I got something for ya both-

-hold on daddy Dub. we'll get to that later, right

now we gone just have some fun-

-yeah, let's have some fun. hoo yaa. get over here and sat on my lap gal-

-don't you wanna see the show we got planned for ya Dub-

-sho, what yaw gone do-

The

moon had cleared the hillside, its eye hardly red at all. a funnel of clouds circling beneath it. the girls presented themselves to each other for Mr. Double, dancing together as the music called out for participants. Arriving at the house Roy and Nathan heard the old man whooping. Pete and Johnny and Troy and the other two boys were hand-tied in the back of the truck. they'd make a nice catch for Dub. Roy and Nathan entered the shack just in time to witness the two girls dancing in their panties and bra in front of a gaping Dub drunk on shine.

-come on in boys yaw just in time to watch the show-

-we got business Dub. got to get over to Alabama before morning-

-sit yourselves down for a moment. have some of this shine this from my private stock-

-we got something for ya. bring'm in Nathan. caught these boys loading up our shine. thought you might want to take a look at'm-

Dub wiped at his eyes as the boys were brought in.

-well, I'll be damn, Johnny what yaw want to steal from me for. and Pete and Troy what I done to you boys. I ain't never done nothing to your folks have I. didn't I talk up for your daddy one night when some men wanted to hurt him?

-what you want us to do with'm-

-why ain't got much choice, theys thieves ain't they-

-now hold on Dub you can't kill me, I'm a white boy. besides this was they idea, I just went along-

-dammit boy is that true-

-that ain't the way of it at all. Johnny and Nan cooked this up-

-Nan? honey was you up in this business. was you? and how about missy Maybelle you got a part in this too? sho, I see it clearly now. yaw get old Dub drunk while these here steal my shine. and you Maybelle what you promise them or what they promise you, take you for a ride away from old Dub. Roy and Nathan how you boys like a turn with these here wenches-

The

little shack could not hold out the sounds of Maybelles' and Nans' screams so Roy and Nathan put a fist to them. Nathan really loved a woman who could kick and scratch. It got deep in his blood and then he would beat them. So, he pounded on Nan with his tool and then he beat her and then he used his tool again. somewhere in the midst of this Nan lost consciousness choking in her saliva and then her life passed from her.

-what you done Nathan. damn look at all that blood-

-Roy what we gone do. what we gone do-

-what the hell you boys doing in here. jeez where all that blood come from? is that gal dead? who did this? I know it was you Nathan been to jail for beating that wife of yours near to death. what you trying to do get everybody locked up. where that Maybelle get to. you fools standing here gaping at that dead gal and let that live one get away, fetch her back here. did yaw beat on her too. if you did I'm gonna kill the both of you-

-come on Pete let's make a run for it while they busy-

-I'm coming with you Troy-

-Johnny you ain't going nowhere with us after what you done. come on Pete—

The

moon's light cast shadows among the trees as

figures emerged from the shack. men running for their lives and Maybelle just running to escape, cutting her exposed nakedness on the brush and branches. watching from above a night owl took a step forward from the cover of his branch at the scene unfolding under him. running from the shack and turning right Maybelle headed for the river. Pete and Troy turned left as they escaped from the shack and ran toward the river.

-shoot them black rascals don't let them get away-

two white men on their way to the river heard the shouting and two or three shots.

-somebody shooting up there!

-sound like they coming this way. get them guns out-

just then Maybelle in all her nakedness appeared in the clearing right in front of them.

-gal what's going on?

Pete and Troy had the misfortune to come running into the same clearing.

-stop right there boy. nigger you here me-

another voice from above the clearing was shouting something.

Maybelle moved out of fear just as the shot rang out. she fell down a hole in her head.

-get down on the ground-

-but we ain't did nothing-

-like hell you ain't you boys is thieves and murderers-

-murderers. we ain't killed nobody-

-shut up. you fellows over there get over here and help us. theys two more boys we caught, they up at Dubs place and a dead white girl they raped and kilt.

Nathan go back with them and bring'm on down here-

-what you want me to do with Johnny?

-bring him too-

Box, a black man fishing on the banks, heard the shooting too and got up and ran along the banks to see what was happening. sometimes you pay dearly for being in the wrong place at the wrong time. Box wished more than a hundred times he had just run across the river when he first heard the shooting but Box had always been one to try and help if he could. when the group of white men with the black boys in tow came upon him they just grabbed him up and carried him along with the others. soon the story became he had been a lookout for the others and it was he that had shot the white girl that had run down the hill trying to get away from Pete and Troy. Never mind that he was still carrying the fishing pole and was known by everyone to have never even owned a firearm of any kind.

The

news of what happened spread quickly. in less than two hours hundreds of white folks had gathered down by the big tree on the other side of the river. the two bodies of the white women lay face down and the four black boys and one white boy were tied up.

Box was hog-tied and silent from the beating he had already received lay on the ground by the wagon.

-Pete what we gone do. man I can't die like this-

-You believe in spirits. in the hereafter-

-I guess-

-can't guess at something like this. I seen my grandfather after he died. came in the house and stood right in front of me. said he had made my Granma a promise he would come and see me one day. he died before I was born. you got to promise yourself you gone come back one day. I'm coming back to see these folks one day. coming back to see they children. visit them like they visiting us now.

yaw hear me. we got to believe that. all of us got to promise to come back here and visit the children of these people-

-we all promise-

The sun was burning hot in the morning. The white folks had hung the four black boys and burned their bodies. they had made a huge bonfire and drank liquor and cursed the dead bodies of the men until the moon's eye had settled under the horizon and the hummingbirds poked their noses into nearby flowers. blood from the swinging corpses fell down into the dew on the grass and the roots of the tree.

Pete and Troy's momma and daddy came by the next day after all the white folks had finally left and retrieved the rotten corpses. the church made noise like usual and the family left town a month later moving up north to Chicago.

part 2

-All the evidence from this case points to all kinds of discrepancies in the original stories. and we even have this written letter found afterwards by Sgt. Molesky that it was unlikely any of these boys had any guns. a white woman on her way to the train remembers seeing Box fishing at the river that same morning around two or three or clock in the morning. the gun that was turned in as evidence belonged to one Nathan Burns one of the white men that just happened to be visiting Mr. Double. He and his brother were known moonshine runners and a truck filled with shine was discovered a week later. the white male Johnny testified that none of them had touched the white women. he was run out of town a year later as a niggah lover. he died ten years later on the Mississippi in a storm. Mr. Double disappeared the morning after the hangings and was discovered in Alaska twenty-two years later. he swore on his death bed to one of two Eskimos at his bedside that the whole thing was a lie about them boys killing his stepchild. we have here a partial letter written in his hand about the truth of the matter. we are asking the state to reopen the case and bring to justice the only surviving known participant in the brutal hanging and burning of the five victims. not one person of the more than two hundred and twenty seven persons at the hangings, including five police officers, was ever charged with any crime. it was as if those men had hung and burned themselves-

-we will consider the matter. this court is adjourned and will reconvene in four weeks-

-four weeks? you mean that yaw just gone let innocent folks sit in their graves with no vindication-

-order. order in my court. bailiff remove that man. court dismissed-

-dammit Troy you just can't do that. you gone prejudice the jury-

-I'm sorry Mr. Newporet but every time I think about what my family been through it drives me crazy. I know what yaw trying to do. if the NAACP's legal team hadn't taken up this fight this would have gone the way of all our other attempts to get this case reopened-

-you got to understand. all of you have got to understand white folks ain't trying to dig up the past. they want all of that stuff that their grandparents, great grandparents did to stay dead. they know eventually it means somebody gone be found guilty and worst of all they know they gone have to pay somebody some money and you know how white folks is when it comes to having to pay out money to some underprivileged black folks-

-you mean angry black folks-

-put any label on it you want. sixty one years ago is sixty one years. we got to let the evidence speak not our anger or frustration-

Troy

was the great grandson of Cisco and Millie. His grandfather was Paul, Troy and Pete's baby brother. the family had migrated to Chicago. Paul had five sons, one of whom he named Troy in memory of his brother. that son had died in the war in Asia. he had never seen his son, also named Troy. grandpa Paul told the story to Troy Jr. or Jolly as they called him because as a baby he was always laughing.

-I seen my brother Troy in a dream one night. he was standing under that big tree where they had hung him. he held up six fingers and then said one day promises will be kept. he looked so peaceful and there was seven female birds flying around him-

-how you know they was female bird's grandpa?

-they said they was-

Last

year the town of Nailpex had suffered the worst spring it had ever experienced. Then came day after day of dry weather. Even winter came and went with no rain or snow. The trees heaved dry leaves and the flowers on the petals refused to blossom. The river Ters barely made it through town.

Nailpex

was celebrating its one hundred and fortieth year. Many of the descendants of the old families were coming to town to celebrate the first week of August.

On

the first night of July seven women, all dressed in white, were seen in the river walking in its waters by the big tree. they walked all night back and forth. not one of them said a word. in the morning they were seen leaving covered with purple cloaks, a trail of dry leaves following them out of town.

A

deep silence set over the town as if the wind were waiting for someone to speak. a few days later someone said they saw a man come out of the ground by the big tree and run up the hill howling. the man who told that story was the town drunk.

-I tell I see him plain as day. popped right out of the ground, dirty and black. he stared at me and said one day and then ran up the hill howling—one day, one day-

-Crily I told you all that drinking was gone drive you crazy. like that time you told us about that midget you saw driving a truck-

-I did. he crashed that truck just like I told you but he got away-

-yeah and nobody never seen that truck or that midget-

-well, it was like I said he come back a few hours later with another man, regular sized and they hitched it up and towed it away-

-yeah and you and what's her name climbed up to the top of the steeple on the church and slid down the backside by the cemetery where five men stood and one of them caught you before you hit the ground-

Storm's Tavern was filled with laughter that night but Crily wasn't convinced.

-what about them women people said they saw dressed in white parading around in the river three weeks ago?

-what about them?

-well, who were they? nobody from around here. seem kinda strange to me folks marching around in a river all night-

-have a drink Crily. your tales ain't scaring nobody but you-

-no, no, I'm through drinking. Ain't had a drop in seven days. I got to think. something ain't right here. no rain. day after day the weather the same as the day before. don't yaw think that's kinda strange?

-no, I don't and if you don't stop with this nonsense I'mmo put you out of here. sheriff get over and talk some sense into Crily. we got a big celebration coming up. just about everybody's kin folks gone be here. white and black. first time we ever had a gathering like this and we ain't gone have you spoiling our good time with all your tall tales about some man coming out of the ground-

-you been drinking Crily or maybe you done switched up and been smoking all that wacky tabacky these young folks been smoking-

-no sir sheriff, sober as a judge-

-well, if that's the case you might be drunk. the case the judge got to hear next month brought up by them lawyers from the NAACP got him pretty stirred up. my grandpa was one of the deputies accused in that whole mess. you'd think that folks would just let all that stuff stay under the ground where it belongs. that was a long time ago, things is different now. look around, blacks and whites together having a good time. you think these folks thinking about that..

maybe one or two but folks is living in there time. how many white gals done married some of these black men and vice versa. hell, I like me a little black tail every now and then when I can get it. hell, the mayor and half the councilmen is black.

we even got a couple Hispanics and three Orientals running things. what happened back then wrong or right could never happen nowadays-

-when did all that stuff, you know them hangings and all, what day did that happen sheriff-

-don't recall the exact day but it was around this time of year I know that much-

-so that's how come some of them boys' family come down here every year fussing around that tree. then they go over to the cemetery on the other side of the river. is it true the mother lost her mind?

-look Crily I don't know what happened to them and to be honest with you I have spent the last two weeks in a court listening to all this and I'm certainly not going to spend my night talking to you about the past. what the hell's the matter with you anyway why ain't you drunk like you usually are-

-I dun seen some things that ain't natural. I cain't drink. did you know that my great uncle was

Johnny, the white boy that was with them the night all that stuff happened-

-dammit Crily that's enuf. Storm give me a drink. now here Crily drink this or so help me god I'm gone run your butt straight to jail-

-what for-

-vagrancy you little varmint, disturbing the peace. I don't know but I'm sure I can come up with something-

-not drinking sheriff. told you something ain't right. I feel it in my bones-

Crily

stepped outside. the first thing he noticed was the wind. kicking up dust and throwing things around. the backs of the trees leaned over and the moon was swallowed up by a huge black cloud that came flying over the top of the hill. Crily barely made it to his little shack on the edge of town. the rain hit hard on the ground. the drops like little spades digging and turning the dry soil, pushing the dry leaves ahead of it. Crily looked out the window at the neon signs, they were just blurs of light blinking off and on. then came the lightening. then the thunder. Nailpex was under a violent attack. Crily focused his eyes on top of the hill. he thought he saw a man leaping in the sky as if he were leading a charge. then he flew down the hillside and disappeared in the waters of the now raging river Ters.

August

first the sky blossomed into a bright blue. The trees drank greedily the rainwater that had fell two weeks early. Nailpex looked like a beautiful painting. Its beds of flowers along the side of the road were full of bright daisies and the daffodils were almost singing. Roses made love with the sun, so did many of the brightly colored perennials. The grass was so green it looked unnatural. The rain had washed away all the dead leaves. The streets sparkled.

-never seen the town look so pretty and clean-

-yeah, it's really beautiful-

-they said the rain did all this-

-yeah-

-but wasn't that more than a week ago-

-yeah, I think it was-

-then why hasn't it gotten dirty again-

-I don't know, I hadn't thought about it actually-

-well, Crily knows don't you Crily. tell these good folks

-don't want to talk about it. give me another drink, got to stay drunk-

-who is that?

-that's just Crily, you know the town drunk. told me a couple days after the storm that he saw a man jump in the river-

-jump in the river? what happened to him?

-Crily said the man just disappeared in the water-

-disappeared? town drunk ... right-

-right-

They

came in town one by one, two hours apart, the
women in purple. The celebration was in full
swing. Children of the children of the town's people
that was alive the night of the hangings. They had
gathered down by the river with their banjos and
guitars and drums and trumpets and radios and
boom boxes. some were taking pictures of family
members while the children ran and played.
booths with all kinds of food and amusements and
men folk huddled in a group here and a group
there talking about the past. Some of the sad
things some of the happy things. The things that
folks talk about when families come together after
many years of separation. after a while the talk got
around to the hangings. It was unavoidable since
they were so near to the big tree.

-do you think anybody will ever know what really
happened-

-don't see that it makes much difference now. all them folks is dead now except one and he damn near dead. senile I hear and crippled up-

the talk on the other side of the river was much more adamant

-o yeah, we suffered. when my great grandparents run out of here, and I mean run. they left here with nothing but kids. didn't know what them crazy white folks might do. lot of yaw's kinfolk left here back then. tomorrow is the day when they killed my uncles and those other three and they tell me old man Box wasn't doing nothing but fishing, had no part in it—

-come on Troy, leave this for the courtroom, you'll get your chance to speak-

-I can't talk in no court room like I can talk here among my own people. Swanzee you our attorney but yo family didn't come from nothing like this. it haunts us still. my great grandmamma lost her mind and my great grandfather worked himself to death. when his cousins couldn't help him anymore he moved the family into a two bedroom apartment. my grandfather raised me and the family never was right. crazy folks. crazy in the blood. his sister took to prostituting to help support the family. yaw remember Jake, gambler and hustler died in jail for armed robbery. ten kids and all except one went straight to shit because the family was tore up inside. it came all the way down to my generation before we finally started to get straight. how do people get off a road made by bad people, liars and murderers? it's like yesterday is still happening today.

-you wrong Troy Jr., because what happened to your family happened to everybody made with this skin. why you think I took this case? I did it as much for your suffering as I did for mine. nobody in our race can hide the pain of a son of our people hung on some lovely tree with the moon going down on his body black from fire and smoking. what the sun think when he comes up and becomes a witness to charred remains-

The

night settled in with the many celebrating. The

women in purple had made their way into the river walking to and fro. when the whistling began it seemed to come from some distance away. then came drops of rain.

-it is beginning, it is beginning-

-what's beginning Crily?

-I don't know but my bones don't feel right-

-I been trying to be real nice Crily. first you're drinking then you stop drinking now you back to drinking again. don't seem to matter much, either way you talk crazy. seen any more men pop out of the ground or disappear in that river?

The

sheriff was as surprised as everyone that turned in the direction of his pointing finger. the seven women were in the river walking to and fro, the purple dresses wet up to their breast. they held hands and made a circle leaned back and whistled.

-what's that noise?

-I don't know. sound like it's coming from the river-

Heads

all over the small town were spun around as the whistling increased. the notes calling them. within minutes all the descendants lined both sides of the river.

a voice came out of the tree, out of the branches and leaves-

-heaven is weeping because her sons are crying

because her daughter's children have been dying

who speaks for them

who on earth weeps for them

the seven women in the river continued whistling and then the water came. drop by drop as if someone were counting beads on a board-

-the heavens weep-

What

could not be possible flashed into existence. The apparitions of hung men, burning men swung slowly on the big tree by the river for all to see.

-promises kept. we have returned. we have brought you the story of all that happened that night. listen-

and the story was told. the lies made known.

the mouths of Maybelle and Nan told it all.

-my name is Troy and I admit I did wrong. the lie of that night increased with time because it was a seed. it is time for the reaping and the end of these generations-

The

whistling of the river women brought a wind that flushed the soul of the town and all the people it contained.

The

moon set back on the hill before it rose. The noise

in the valley finally subsided. The river Ters washed away all the remains. When the stars started to move again they followed the path of the seven women out of Nailpex.

-they said it was just the strangest thing that ever happened. what do you supposed really ever happened to them people?

-the government won't talk about it. a man named Crily kept telling some story about dead men returning and taking the whole town-

-the whole town?

-don't nobody listen to him. he's just a drunk.

-well, I like the one about the alien abductions-

-or devil's triangle-

-I knew this old black lady, some folks said she was some kind of voodoo woman. anyway she said god don't like ugly. she told me a story about how this tree white folks used for hanging had shook itself from the ground one night and killed a hundred white folks. all children of the seven men responsible for the hangings-

-when was that-

-a few years ago-

-say fella I got to go. it's been real nice talking with you, by the way what's your name-

- my name is Troy but my nickname is PK-

-what that stand for-

-promises kept-

REMIX of PROMISES KEPT: CELEBRATION

(you know some stories have more than one ending, an alternate universe of events that keep spiraling out of one another-this is one)

-a doctor down by the river, past the bend? healed a pecan tree? what kind of nonsense you telling me Crily. are you drunk again?

-no no. I didn't see it with my own eyes. the Johnson boy told me-

-you mean the one spends most of the day down at the barbershop lying all day about one thing after another? why he ain't nothing but a liar– a comedian for crying out loud-

-well, Ms. Mary said he wasn't laughing when he told her the story and took her up to see for herself-

-gospel Mary the one that totes around that ten-pound bible with the pictures in it. gospel Mary that stands on the corner of every street seven days telling anybody who'll listen that they going straight to hell-

-that's the one-

-any other characters you want to tell me about that seen this miracle. that tree been dead for fifty years. I do believe it's done turned into stone that's why it ain't just fell down-

-now that you mention there was one other person who saw the tree and he even picked some of the pecans off the tree he was so amazed-

-and who the hell was that-

-Bob, the one that runs the meat house-

-cross eyed Bob! what the hell was he doing out there?-

-one of the cows he was getting ready to slaughter broke and run and he had to chase it, him and Marlina Mallory and a couple of boys-

-they saw the pecan tree too-

-no Ms. Mallory said when she saw that doctor

with them seven women and all of them dressed in white with blood red shoes on she couldn't get her foot to go across the town limit-

-you know Crily I been trying to be real patient with you. is there any particular reason you didn't tell me about this doctor and the seven women before now?

-no, I guess I hadn't got to that part of the story with the way you keep interrupting me and all-

-so what happened next Crily-

-well, nobody could get they feet to go past the town limit except Bob. he caught up with the cow at the pecan tree. that's when he said he first took notice of the man and the women. he said when he looked in the man's face he couldn't see the man's eyes. he asked the man what he was doing there and he said the man said he was a doctor come to heal the sick and the dying. Bob said the man's voice didn't sound right, like the words were caught in his throat and each word he spoke came out like a hiss, like a snake or something. scared old Bob good-

-and Johnson he say the same thing?

-yeah. that's why he was so scared. said the man and the women didn't look like regular people. what kind of doctor you think he might be running around in a white suit and blood red shoes and hat?

-he had on a hat. you didn't tell me about the hat-

-anyway, a whole lot of the townspeople done run up the road but most of them feet won't go across the town limit-

-you mean to tell me all this time you been standing here in front of me telling this half the town has gone up the road-

-yeah, and most of them just stuck up there-

-what the hell you mean stuck?

-well, they just stuck. can't go forward and they can't go backward. a few of them made it out of town but they couldn't go no further than the pecan tree which is just dropping pecans as fast as the people pick'um up-

-shut up Crily, don't say another word. I done wasted ten good minutes listening to you. let's go-

When

the sheriff got halfway up the road leading out of town he saw the crowd. most of them had the most confused look on their faces he had ever seen. It was like the look of a diabetic whose sugar had run low. with the town behind them he reached the sign that read town limit and found his feet also could not cross the line but Crily kept walking right over to the pecan tree not more than a hundred feet away.

There

 in the cool shade of the now spitting tree stood the doctor just as Crily described him, tall, lean, kind of swaying in the slightest breeze as if he had no body weight, dressed in a white suit with a doctor's white leather bag instead of black and the seven women and all of them with blood red shoes and hats on. the sheriff couldn't figure why his feet no longer worked as he and the others stood stuck on the road as if time had stopped.

The

doctor seemed to be in no particular hurry. But the women seemed to be working themselves into a frenzy, dancing around the tree and whistling the strangest tune. More people of the town came up the road until the whole town was empty. Called there by the doctor and whistling vixens.

The

doctor opened his bag and pulled out a bloody hangman's rope. The dance of the women was approaching a crescendo as they slipped around and around the tree.

-None of you know me but your ancestors knew the night of lies to protect a way of life almost dead. But we promised we would return so that the truth could be told. Now, I want all of you to join me now down at the river and see for yourselves the past come to life-

The

doctor and the dancing women headed down to the river and the people of the town followed. They gathered at the river, all of them descendants of Nailpex.

The

night fell over them and the moon stayed back looking from the other side of the hill, its face dusty and brown from the clouds of pollution hanging in the air.

The

doctor went to the tree by the river and the descendants of Nailpex arranged themselves into generations by race and age and association on the banks of the river. Blacks here, whites there and the young ones mixed in like flowers. Standing next to the large old tree the doctor pointed to an area above the water as he spoke.

-This is the tree of misery, swollen with the screams and tears and blood of men guilty and innocent. But it has anger that it cannot contain and it has been pregnant with this seed for many years until today. Now, it has a child. It has children. All the seeds spit out by the pecan tree, a dead thing made alive to cleanse away some of the old things. Look there in the air and see the truth-

Above

the river on a screen flashed all the events of what happened the night Troy and his brother were hung and the killing of Nan and Maybelle. The women in white were in the river chanting and dancing, churning the water and whirling in a dervish spin. More images of other lies and hangings slid on the screen only to be replaced by other tragedies. The people on both sides of the banks of the river cried for different reasons and asked for forgiveness for what had been done.

-This evil must be cleansed. No trial of man can end this. This is the way. All of you generations old and new must join me now. You must go away from this world-

The

seven women began to whistle loudly whipping the

river Ters into a frenzy and the tree of misery reached out its limbs and gathered all into its bosom. The swollen river swallowed them all.

The

moon rose from behind the hill and sped to its apex, silvery and bright. The evening star danced into a position just under the moon as a crowd of noise approached from the other heavenly players, Venus and Mars, Betelgeuse and Sirius and thousands of extras.

-It was in all the newspapers and you mean you didn't hear nothing about it. Where you been mister off the planet?

-Yeah, something like that. So, they never found any evidence that this river had ever flooded before? Suddenly rising over its banks and destroyed the whole town?

-Yeah, but the whole thing is really weird. First off they don't know where all the water came from-

-What d'ya mean?

-Well, there weren't any storms reported in that area.

-Then they found a live pecan tree with all these pecans around it, I mean thousands of them.-

-What's strange about that?

-Man, where you from, don't you know nothing? Pecan trees don't drop their pecans until late fall. October, November, that was in August-

-uumph-

-uumph. That's all you can say. Let me tell you the weirdest thing of all though. They can't find any of the people, not one. Not a single bone. Nothing. Some people think it was aliens. Maybe some kind of advance party sent here to steal some of us and take us back to their crappy world and poke around in us-

-You think-

-I'll tell you this, the government's real concerned, they got military people up there investigating the whole thing. There was this one survivor...-

-I thought you said nobody survived-

-Well, this guy, Crily is his name, he was the town drunk. They found him drunk in another town a week later talking crazy about some doctor all dressed in white with these blood red shoes on and white medical bag and seven whistling women in purple hats and white dresses. He keeps telling this story about some dead guy named Troy that came back and took out his vengeance on the town for hanging him and his friends a hundred years ago-

-And you don't believe that do you?

-Are you nuts, hell no. Hey, wait a minute you leaving? I ain't finished telling you the rest of the story-

-No, I think I've heard enough-

-You know I just realized you wearing a white suit and you got on blood red shoes. You in a band or something?

-So, I do and I even have a doctor's bag, a white one-

-Where are your women, outside dancing?

Laughter

came across the bar like a wave as some of the patrons listening to the conversation watched the man in white heading for the door.

-That's the guy that drunk Crily keeps talking about. I told him to go outside and bring his girls in-

Others

in the bar joined in the laughter with the big man that had been talking to the guy in white. The laughter faded as the sound of whistling snaked its way through the door into the soul of the men in the bar. Too late for any of them to move. Too late for the town of Mirerrs-

-you never told me your name?

-my name is PK-

-what does that stand for?

-Promises Kept-

...my God she is rare...

OPEL

The

face flowed behind each thought. We all knew she was near. Felt the presence of her oncoming steps like the swell of the waves lapping the shore. Each year additional turns of suitors spun their words, gathered about her porch. The house within strewn with presents.

The

face of Opel they all adored had become an ocean, with a liquid surface. The suitors entangled in their lines. Never witnessed such ceaseless fishers but Opel was always kind. My eyes felt magnetized too. Nothing hard in my look. Nothing hard in her look. An understanding quietly took a seat. Slowly the others peeled themselves off. I felt as though I had been blessed above all men.

She

was in the shower the first time I saw her flesh. Her face held a ray of sunlight. The view was lovely. Her skin was smooth tissue, an unmanned wilderness that had evolved into a wild beauty. For days afterwards I was dazzled. At the barbershop men asked me about the affair with Opel. There was no resentment in their sound, no jealousy in my vision. Understand that Opel was special in the eyes of men. She possessed us all without touching because she sensed the heart. I didn't mention the day I saw her skin. A boy of seventeen wondered about the beauty of my smile. It was then that we all noticed the change in me.

I

returned that evening to Opel. The room was blaring from the light and noise of the TV. Opel went to sleep with the fringe darkness draped over her. I was too tired to go on.

I

awoke crumpled in a chair. Opel was rubbing my

legs back to life. Through the window I saw an animal feeding in the brush. We sat on her porch and ate raisins. Her garden had grown at least three inches in a week.

Around

midday she went to her mother's. She was gone for hours. Her mother called at six. She was gone for hours. I was sure it was the other men. I sat on the porch and watched the moon come up. She came down the walk. She took the other chair, folded her legs over the woody arms and whistled.

-your mother called-

-I was with my Mother-

-your mother called at six-

-my mother is life. here. there. The river on ol' Pete's farm or the cherry tree down in the valley. It is simply a matter of the come and go.

My

anger passed slowly. Opel was a wave. How do you get to know a wave? There was little doubt in my mind that she was not in the hands of men.

Opel

was a huge virgin. Huge because of the ocean that moved within her, vast and liquid and she flowed over the ice in January. Her red skates aflame. We held hands that day. Her skin and movements, the wind, the eyes of the other men. I was with the stars that night.

Somewhere

in the world several nations were at war. For the next three years I was a war correspondent. Opel sent a letter– I only read your news, only yours– The world was still trying to die in August. The war ended abruptly. I sent for her that October. We occupied a room on the coast of Africa. I thought she was beautiful. Other men beheld her face. Poets unearthed images with their words and painters attacked their canvasses to hold still for her liquid glo. This affair had plunged old and young alike to discover a way to capture her essence in art.

We

arrived in New York. The jazz trumpets were angelic. I drew closer for fear that soon she would evaporate. She glowed for the world and I loved her more. I had never possessed another woman. She was not that kind. Our romance was not the bruising kind.

Life

with Opel was a film. All the bad shots cut out, leaving a finished product that exhibited the potential of the soul. My smile had grown until it covered my body. Again I felt blessed, I was part of the show.

The

highlights of New York paid our way into the highest circles. The beautiful country girl and the war correspondent, entertainment for the delight of the rich peoples' souls. They thought she only knew the world barefoot. They sat as we entered, applauding themselves for their wealth. We sat in silence for three hours. The sun sank and yet the quiet of Opel flowed like a wave, imperceptible as the smallest dancing ripple. A flower without legs so beautiful she seemed to beg to be moved. I watched as the guests gathered, hypnotized by this flame, this wave so new, so complete it swept them from their seats. For many of them it was the first time silence had quieted them down. Opel was influence and I smiled, smiled until I felt a wave wash through me on to them. I became airy. The guests were silent. Another wave and it washed out onto the street. Opel held us all. It was magnetism. She stood up, this huge virgin put her hand in mine and announced

-we're going to my mother's-

I

can tell you now that Opel was divine. I never touched her. She was not the kind for brutality. She was a wave to set you aflame. She was truly her mother's child and I feel blessed having known she was so.

... what a mean world this can be...

DOG FIGHT

Three

days of snow and now a vicious rainstorm. Cleveland is too moist, I thought to myself. I pushed the Chrysler 300 through a large puddle, passed two vehicles, darted on an inside lane, cursed several pedestrians and said out loud

- Where in the hell did these people get their driver's licenses Woolworth's?

-You ain't got to change colors do ya? the wife said.

The

first words to break a fifteen-minute silence. I ignored her comment. It had taken fifteen years and countless arguments for me to learn not to reply to her when she used that tone. It meant endless talking. I had no desire for the inner turmoil that followed our battles so I let silence occupy my mouth.

Our

relationship had changed and settled down in a place that was acceptable to both of us as long as it remained within the confines we had agreed on as the boundaries not to venture past. Trial and error is a mother. The innocence and sweetness of love a thing of the past. It ended the day she made some reference to light-skinned dudes being closer to white men than dark-skinned dudes. I exploded.

-How many light-skinned dudes got to die before this bullshit stops. White folks look at Malcolm X, Ali and Rosa Parks with the same feeling as they do any other colored man. Damn white folks fucked you up-

We

settled down into a nasty ten year war because she always had to have the last word. It had caused us to drift to others, another circumstance and reason for warfare. We learned to live with a lot and even found time to make babies and a home.

-You just passed the arena-

She brought me back to the present.

-Damn-

I made a quick u-turn. It took fifteen minutes to park. We were an hour late as usual. I didn't mind too much though because I was only interested in the main attraction anyway. The girl that took our tickets had large oval brown eyes. They gathered me up. Time makes a man appreciate young girls. Her fingers were very pliable. We exchanged a silent greeting. I decided to smile. Her eyes shifted to my wife's. An awkward silence ensued. Someone in the line said something obscene.

-thank you— She said, her tongue slipping out of her mouth.

-thank you– I replied.

Smoke,

perfume, and the smell of sweat filled the main

corridor. We took the up ramp in front of us to the second level and got to our seats. Man it was one of those electric nights. Stars in the sky, the moon coming up over the open end of the stadium, blood red. A poet friend of mine, Pete, once wrote "all young girls are fine and all old men know it." Well, thank god I hadn't gotten that old when everybody younger than me looked like babies. I think Tiah still considered me to be some kind of juvenile. Hey, I like looking at women, especially sisters. I don't get mad when she looks at brothers and then she even has the nerve to say shit like:

-That brother got on a bad outfit-

I

know what that means, but what the hell don't nobody own nobody. So at some point we just stopped pretending other people didn't exist and a look was just a look. Well, up to a certain point but you supposed to use some kind of common sense.

The

stadium was packed, filled to capacity. These

damn tickets cost one hundred and fifty dollars. Tiah thought I had lost my mind. I explained to her that this was a once-in-a-lifetime event and I wasn't about to miss it.

-I'll pay the light bill next week-

The crowd roared as the fighters were introduced. A speaker was right over our section.

-weighing 160 pounds the middleweight champeen of the world Hudi Jabar-

The crowd drowned out the announcer.

The challenger Joe Thomas was undefeated in 29 bouts. Joe had tiny slits for eyes and a muscular body. They were the same weight and height and Hudi had a slight reach advantage of two inches.

Joe looked across the ring and made a face at Hudi, shaking his face like a lion. The bell sounded. The fight was underway. They touched gloves. Joe tried an overhand right that grazed Hudi backing away.

-get 'um Joe—

-knock his teeth out-

The

fans were yelling, all of them, forgetting all about how they had dressed for the occasion. The money people down front craned their necks backwards to see the action. Taking my eyes from the fight I don't think I had ever seen that many brilliant colors; orange leathers, white furs, diamonds, gold, and pearls. You name it folks was wearing it. Women and men all juiced up for this grind. Look at what the Romans had created. The frenzy of the crowd growing as round six ended. Jabar ahead on points but it was one of those fights where both men had already taken a lot of punishment.

Round 7.

Jabar came out fast. His corner was yelling instructions:

-Pick up the pace, use your left hook, hook-

Joe's corner was an echo of similar instructions.

-Counter right hook, straight left over his right, dig

underneath-

Sweat

was beading on Joe's side. Jabar moved in. Joe slid to the left. Jabar threw his best punch, a short right as Joe waded in. Joe countered with two lefts to the body. Jabar clinched. Referee Hank Moseley, a former heavyweight fighter, separated them. Jabar connected with two jabs to the head. A looping right hand to the body. Two more jabs and a right. Joe went into the ropes. Jabar followed with a left-right combination.

The crowd was on its feet again going crazy.

Joe came back with a wicked right to the head. The fighters clinched again. Joe dug into Jabar with a low blow. Jabar backed away, his back to the referee blinding Joe's punch. Joe was on him with another right to the head. Another right and Jabar looked dazed. The bell sounded.

Money was passing hands rapidly after that. A couple of arguments and fights broke out. Right behind us two men exchanged a few blows and then some big white security cops broke it up and hauled the drunken men out.

Jabar listened intensely to his instructions. Joe was countering his right leads with left hooks but going to his right when he pulled out.

-Fake the right to draw him in. When he counters with his right step inside and nail him. Let's go home champ.

The bell rang for round ten.

Jabar came out dancing. Joe was on him. The tempo of the fight had increased as both fighters tried to dominate the other but neither giving an inch. Joe landed a powerful overhand right and Jabar's knees buckled. He stopped dancing and backed up. Joe followed with two shots to the body. They exchanged rights. Joe missed with a wild right as they fought against the ropes. Jabar fought back and walked Joe back to the center of the ring and then landed a sweet body shot. Joe again struck low, his third one of the night. Moseley sent Joe to a neutral corner. Pointing to the judges he raised his finger for a point deduction. Joe's corner went bananas. Jabar's face showed the pain of the low blow and the fight. The bad blood between the camps took on a different tone. Somebody in the crowd yelled dog fight. The whole stadium took up the chant.

-dog fight! dog fight!!-

You couldn't hear yourself think it was so loud. They wanted blood.

The

fight had become a war, a gladiator event. Tiah did not really like fights and this was being shifted into a dark corner. It was the spectacle of being there. In the twelfth round Jabar landed a low blow of his own.

Round thirteen.

Tiah was holding my hand tightly. The fury of the battle gripped the audience and the chant dog fight started up again. Everybody had begun to inch forward. Some guy with a radio had come down from above us and I could hear the radio announcer:

-Jabar with a left to the head, oooh what a right by Joe. Folks you have to be here to believe this. This has been pure dynamite. The crowd has gone absolutely crazy. Oh boy, there's another hard right and a left. I've never seen anything like this. Joe just caught Jabar coming in with a hard left, now another left, they're whacking each other something terrible. They're right over us now, their faces twisting as the shots land. I don't know how either of them is still standing-

-I have hit this guy with everything and he keeps coming– Joe breathed heavily in his corner.

-I know Joe, just keep hitting him. Keep your hands up-

Round fourteen opened with the crowd pushing its way forward. A human tidal wave trying to get as close to the action as possible. One second I had Tiah's hand, the next I lost sight of her completely. I tried to buck the crowd but it was useless.

-Dog fight dog fight dog fight-

The

ear was pierced fatally, the crowd wanted blood, they wanted a victim. The urging of the crowd sent energy into the men warring on center stage. The crowd was now a pack. I looked up into the sky for relief. A funny shaped cloud stood in position right in front of the moon. I went back to the crowd. Pleasure and pain lit up their faces. This was a brutal war between half-clad men. A woman I stared at had her hands in her pants her face flushed with sexual fever, the pleasure of war.

Both

fighters were bleeding. They went at each other in a final assault. Joe yelled something and Jabar answered with a left-right combination that left Joe in deep trouble. Joe tried to clinch but Jabar backed away tossing an uppercut at Joe that caught him flush. Joe staggered into the ropes. Jabar struck him six times and Joe went down. The crowd climaxed.

Joe was up at the count of seven his legs unsteady. Jabar went in to for the kill.

From the radio I heard:

-Joe's in real trouble now. Oh what a right. Joe's back against the ropes in his own corner. Another uppercut, Joe's leaning back, catches a right, a left, another left, they're going to stop this... oh there's another hard right, Joe's head is rolling, Jabar is desperately trying to finish him off. Two body shots, Joe's got to be done for, Jabar looks at the referee, no action from the referee, Jabar clubs Joe with a vicious shot to the head.. Joe's down Joe's down. This fight is over.

The noise from the crowd was deafening.

Joe was in a heap on the canvass.

The doctor was in the ring. Joe hadn't moved. Jabar's head was hanging through the ropes. Something was wrong. One of Joe's corner men was in the middle of the ring, I couldn't hear him but he was pointing his finger at Jabar's corner. The bad blood between the fighters' camps spilling over.

I had to find Tiah, get the hell out of here. This was turning ugly. The crowd was turning ugly. More fights had broken out. I finally got out into the main corridor.

Tiah was up against the wall pressed there by the mass exodus. I caught up to her and we made our way outside.

-What the hell is wrong with these people?

-Tiah I don't know, crazy I guess-

-Is that why you was yelling dog fight with the rest of those idiots-

-Was I yelling dog fight, naw I don't think so-

-Yeah you were. You should have seen your face. Did you know that man died in there tonight-

I

turned on the radio as soon as we got into the 300.

-It has been confirmed here at ringside that Joe Thomas died in the ring tonight after one of the most vicious fights ever seen-

I felt sick.

-You know what Turnlo, take me to an afterhours club, ok. I want to be drunk when you ask me to make love to you tonight.

...games for adults...

MILLION DOLLAR TASTEE

-give me liquid, give me little liquid-

The

audience clapped and yelled. Both contestants' heads were deep in the viewer screen. The phrase flashed across and an audio voice repeated at high speed one of the words from the phrase. Each correct word was placed at the top of the screen but out of order. The contestants were in soundproof plastic booths and spoke into audio receivers used the keyboard to type their answer. So even if they guessed the word correctly they had to spell it correctly. It was the most popular game show in history.

The

game had ten levels with a minimum of fifty thousand with five correct answers. The top prize was one million dollars. The show had been on three years and only two people so far had claimed the top prize. If you went thru all ten levels a contestant could win a total of three and a half million dollars or you could skip straight to level ten by completing the first five levels without a miss and still win the prizes from level six thru level nine.

Al

cruised along at ninety miles an hour. They hardly noticed the desert whizzing by outside the air-conditioned caddy. In the distance lay large snow-topped mountains or were those clouds?

Mountains are lazy, Al thought to himself.

Barbara slid into the scenes of their last winnings. They had won the caddy, fifty thousand dollars in cash, a trip to Mexico and other items for their house. All this in less than eighteen months.

-your little liquid, let the liquid fall-

Al

had lost four different jobs in two years. The economy had gone screwy. He was dissatisfied. She was dissatisfied. He enjoyed fooling around, making wood items but never really had the time or the money for it. Al was between jobs when the answer came to a letter he had written a few months ago. He was accepted as one of the contestants on the Concert Game Show. He went on the show and won.

Barbara

was next. It was July when she appeared on the Pyramid Game Show. She walked off the show with ten thousand dollars and a trip to the Caribbean.

Europe

was next. Al and Barbara had discovered a fantastic lifestyle: game shows. Nearly all of the developed countries of the world had some type of game show. They discovered to their surprise that only a few people in the world had discovered this new job. They became professionals. It was a long way from scrabble and two dollars a word in their former inner-city lifestyle. Their pictures were in newspapers.

The

show they were on now only allowed contestants that had won on some other game show. Their competitors were John and Joyce who had been playing game shows for about three years. They had met them originally in Brazil a year ago and lost to them on another show, taking second place.

-give me liquid, give me liquid– John rushed the words out typing them. They appeared on the boards of both contestants' screens. They had two words—give me—.

Al studied the viewer as it flashed the phrase again. He saw give me—and made out the letter l but couldn't see the rest of the phrase. He checked the time-twenty-five seconds left. Damn this is the craziest game they had ever played.

This was Barbara's idea, her plan for what she called a *'Million Dollar Tastee'*. 21 seconds left. They hadn't missed a phrase and skipped directly to level ten. Three and a half million dollars. Al and John's wife watched on the monitor, neither of them could figure out the phrase. If their husbands couldn't figure it out they all went home empty-handed, that was the penalty if you skipped from level five to level ten.

Al had talked to Barbara before the show,

-why don't we just take what we have won so far. We got a hundred thousand guaranteed.

-what about my *'Million Dollar Tastee'* you promised me?

-that was before I realized how hard this game is, damn Barbara there is a point when we need to accept what we got. Don't you like the traveling, the free prizes. The hundred thousand is enough money for us to go into our own business. You know the light don't shine on you forever. We need to take advantage of the time and opportunity these games have given us-

-yeah there is a time. But Al remember how things used to be. No money, changing jobs all the time. We may not ever get another chance like this-

-What do you mean, there must be a hundred game shows out there-

-Yeah and we been on at least twenty in different countries. We're professionals, at least that's how they're gonna look at us. Pretty soon we might not be able to get on any of these shows-

-I hadn't thought about that. Ok Barbara. But if were going to win this you need to go first, you're always good at opening the show. You open and I'll close-

-Deal-

Al studied the phrase intensely-the missing word was not liquid, it was, it was light!

-let your little light shine, let your little light shine-

Al yelled into the monitor and typed the phrase.

-Mr. Stamms you've done it, you've done it-

The audience went wild. Barbara nearly knocked Al to the ground when he came out of the booth. They both jumped up and down as balloons and confetti rained down upon them. Lights on the staged flickered.

-go, go, go, go, go, go-Al and Barbara repeated over and over.

Calming things down for a moment the host of the show Tom Topping, presented them with an oversize check of three million dollars and prizes including trips to Hong Kong, Ethiopia, Thailand, a boat they had won and a red Thunderbird.

Al looked out the window and watched the landscape of the desert whizzing by.

For them the games had ended as they fixed the red Thunderbird on the horizon and drove in the direction of a set of eastern stars making an appearance in the rising night sky.

... change the future work hard in the days you are alive...

CLOWNS

She

looked into his eyes a long time. Her hand wandered off. Willie wasn't surprised when he found it. He kissed her. Their auras turned red with passion. Pink lips showed themselves through hair. They puckered up. He lost his hands in her hair. Outside the circus was grinding to a halt. They never heard above their sounds. Their bodies wound up. She pushed him back against the bed and his nose fell off. He slipped out of his outfit. Betty gave his eyes her deepest look. This would be the third time they made love.

-I love this guy-

-I love this girl-

The

outfits tumbled to the floor. He messed with her titty. She messed with him. He held her behind and rubbed it hot. She rotated and him with it. It was hot against his skin. Betty was moving real slow and hard. He moved hard against her. He poked her five times. She smelled his body. His nose was wide open. Sweat poured down her face. Willie saw Betty's eyes. They were wild. His left hand wiped away the sweat. Betty's brown skin contrasted against the white make up. She kissed Willie's ear. They ground out on the bed. He poked her. He poked her. She swallowed him deeper than before. There was so much moisture it flowed. She flowed.

Willie

was her black man. He was full of common sense and had spirit. When they joined like this she felt him in her mind and she responded. A man like Willie made life fuller, happier. So much more worthwhile.

-Hey Happy you seen Willie? the circus manger asked.

-Yeah, with Betty, in the wagon-

-Hey you clowns wake up in there— the circus manager said smiling. He didn't care if they were black. They were funny. That's all that mattered to him.

-by the way I like that new routine-

Betty felt good. She slipped her hand on Willie.

Black

folks had come a long way so they could have life a little better. That morning they thanked their American ancestors. They worked hard. They worked very hard.

....the benefit of time...

2

-**S**it down over there boy and I'll try to explain it to you. We living in the times of fever. Everybody got a touch of it. You know the money's bad. Black folks seem to always find themselves on the steps with their heads in their hands. What I'm trying to say boy, is that a black man got so many wars to fight that he don't need one that really ain't worth dying for-

The

boy looked at him with a black face.

-Well, look at it this way. Men fight the world in different ways. I don't want you to misunderstand me. I means you got to struggle so you can survive but some fighting to me is unnecessary. Look. Black folks fight white folks some kinda way every day. They still think they own us. (stands) And they expect us to go fight some more poor people our own color, suffering like we do, oppressed. It's money boy, it's always about the money. Don't ever forget that my daddy told me that and he was right. I told them I wasn't going to his war. So, they put me in jail. That's why it took so long for me to come home.

There was a tear in the boy's eyes.

-You ashamed of me boy? I know you hear people talking. Boy, there ain't no glory in putting on a uniform that tells the world you're a killer in the name of your country. Especially if the people you doing it for don't love you. Men came back from that war and couldn't even live in the same neighborhood with white folks. Go to their schools, work on the same jobs, killed some of them for trying to vote. There is no glory in war. Men fight wars because of greed. This world is home. What is all the wars in history meant to the poor? Nothing but more misery. We have to learn to accept one another for what we are, to share not take. It's just a fever boy, just a fever that's passing around trying to make some weak soul all churned up inside.

-but daddy you and mommy still fight-

The

reverend reached over and hugged his son

-we're still learning son, we're still learning.

TOMMY

Tommy

had been sitting on the porch for almost an hour. Occasionally a bird would sing out. He followed the sound down the small hill street until it was swallowed by the larger sounds of the city. For him it was the only reason he still lived in the house.

It

had been a strange day so far. Georgia had stopped running her mouth and there hadn't been a single breeze since he had been on the porch. His eye watched the tree. He had only one good eye now. Five months ago he had lost the use of his left eye in a chemical explosion at the plant. The right eye was damaged; most of the swelling had gone down. The doctor assured him they could surgically repair the cornea. His legs were another matter, nerve damage couldn't be determined and he would definitely walk with a limp.

Nine months to go.

Overhead

a familiar cloud was still at attention. A cloud motionless in the sky for an hour?

-Damn don't seem like that's possible– Tommy spoke out loud in his new gravelly voice.

He rocked the chair back against the front of the house to the left of the living room window. Chips of paint fell. Tommy rocked the chair forward and put his mouth against the screen door to his right nearly toppling the chair. He found the extra weight he had gained affecting his balance lately.

-gonna have to paint before the winter sets in-

Nothing. No voice. No wind. No answer.

Tommy

had nothing to do. Five months of sitting. He had gained over twenty pounds adding to his already bulging stomach.

Full height-five nine with a meaty head on top.

Tommy

had always carried a full body. Georgia always said she would get her a man with a full body. Tommy wanted a woman, he got Georgia. He also inherited a mouth, relentless in its pursuit of talk. Tommy had always enjoyed being alone. It had begun, hidden at first, then right there in his mind vivid emotions. At night, late talking along with the talk show, in the morning through the morning talk show. Talking so much on the phone, to neighbors. Tommy placed a reminder over his lips not to start any conversations.

Recently

he began to feel himself sinking. His former life shattered, coming all over his tomorrow. His life today had as much energy and purpose as a wet rag. Tommy was limp. Georgia said . . . Georgia thinks . . . Georgia knows . . .

What!!

She

confused his manhood. Women like Georgia confused a lot of men's manhood. She didn't care about his disability. She didn't care that he wasn't working just now. She complained about his sexual performances and his lack of conversation. Now there was more slipping in her conversation, something she said the other morning.

-That's right. I wish to god you would grow up. I wish all you men would grow up. Geraldene was right, men can dish it out but they can't take it-

-What the hell you talking about. I just asked you to help me with the chair-

-Ok and who' gonna help me in the kitchen. How about making up the bed or vacuuming, no wonder I can't have a baby. I done ripped something from all this work I do or you just spitting water-

-Dammit Georgia you ain't gonna stop this shit are you. We both know I got a low sperm count-

-That don't make no difference, it's activity that counts-

-Now hold on who the fuck you think you talking

to-?

-I'm talking to yo ass. I'm Georgia-wide and green. Your problem is that women nowadays is different. Not like our mothers. We got feelings. But you, you sitting out there on that porch or watching me like I'm the dumbest thing walking, pretending you a man. You ain't just crippled in your eye you need a mental adjustment. Keep talking about painting. Keep on taking time off from life and see if you see what you think you seeing-

-Let me tell you something woman I can see damn well with this one eye. I married you 'cause you wasn't like my momma or any other woman I had messed with. But goddamn you just can't up and change the whole world over night. If it wasn't for men none of you so-called new women would be so new. Shit the whole thing is all screwed up nowadays. Women with women acting like men and men chasing men what kind of crap is that? Maybe we can't have no baby but that ain't no reason for you to act so hateful is it? I tell you what if you tired of this you need to get the hell on-

-It's easier for men than it is for women but women have changed. I was born this way. I can't explain why I feel this way. It's a change I can't resist. If you don't understand then we ain't gonna be together-

Tommy and Georgia, their marriage a downhill story. Georgia led herself into the city three months later. She began another life.

Tommy

had nothing to do. He finished thirty years at the plant. After a life of sitting. No breezes in his life. Tommy was in a tree far from the main river. His head on the earth. He bore no fruit. He didn't flower in the spring. Tommy died one day his head empty. Nothing had killed him.

...whose mind is it...

SNAPSHOT 2

1.

There

is such an infinity of space as we pass over each note of music. The distance between her hand on her oh naked half of ass and the folded skin lips. Roll back this tissue and gape at the pink juices expiring into space.

I'm

dreaming at the wheel and there is so much space in the notes' insistence. Dare the light of the sun fail? Insistence. Insistence as the distance of things. Were it not for pressure pressuring we would seldom meet only collide like raindrops in a free fall to earth. Insistence: the orange song. Pour some liquid in space and stop clinging to the walls. Street pedestrians are in for an ending. Let's break it up. The highway is wide open.

2.

An

hour later the sun was singing. We were both right. Insistent space is everywhere everywhere; over hill over dale. The utter note that eludes the dying mouths of horses and sea urchins. All these notes are insistent. From back of the limo I tell her over the com:

-Drive on please-

Ted and Alice watched from the third floor of the yellow mansion. Alice goes to the bed.

-They're leaving-

-Good. You and your brother make me nervous-

-It's just an interest we have in each other's affairs, that's all-

-Oh look, now don't start that shit again, Ted. You act like two freaks. How do you always know where your brother is? It's creepy. Like that time he walked in on us in that cave at three o'clock in the morning, with grape juice. How did he know I wanted that? I've heard about being telepathic but you two have taken this to another level-

-Alice, I'm not sure if you could understand-

-Yes, but Ted what kind of relationship can we expect to have if we don't talk about this?

-Ok let's talk-

Ted got in the bed. Alice got in the bed.

-You've been acting a little strange tonight. Like that time you and that twin of yours switched places with each other after we left that restaurant. I almost got into bed with that fool. If he hadn't been laughing so hard there's no telling what might have happened. Lean over so I can feel your chin. Since you two grew those little short beards I can't tell you apart-

Alice's fingers smoothed back the hair on Ted's chin feeling the small lump of skin that protruded ever so slightly. Time and space, the notes of insistence. Damn the consequences it's only circumstantial evidence for the non-believers.

-Alice what I'm going to tell you you may not believe. Bob and I were part of a study when we were children, on twins and their feelings. It's pretty common for twins to feel some of the same things at the same time. Bob and I have that and more.

-What do you mean more?

-Bob and I have rather unusual minds. It seems that distance or time has no meaning for us-

-You mean that you guys have telepathic powers-

Alice was smiling.

-The government did a study on us and paid us rather well. Occasionally we go on missions-

-So, you work undercover for the government?

Alice's sense of relief was obvious.

-Well, I know how to keep a secret, Ted. If you have to be gone for a while I can always tell my family that you are out of town on business-

-I'm sorry Alice I'm explaining this badly. The reason Bob knew where we were that night in the cave is because he was already there-

-What do you mean he was already there? You mean he was hiding there?

-No, I mean he was there . . . I mean we were both there . . . were always together, always-

Alice got out of the bed looking at Ted's face.

-What do you mean "you're always together"?

-I told you you wouldn't understand. The people at the study didn't believe it either at first. They believe it now-

-What are you trying to tell me, Ted?

-Ted and I share the same mind Alice-

-Are you trying to tell me that you guys are so

telepathic that you can kinda tune into each other whenever you want?

-No, it's more than that-

Alice's face fell as the creepiness of what she was hearing was more than she could believe. She went over to the window. Looking in the distance she could see the lights of Bob's limo going over the hill.

-Is Bob here now?

-Yes-

-That's impossible, isn't it?

-Not for us. That's what I'm trying to explain to you. It's what the scientist couldn't believe. Ted and I have the same mind. One mind that we live in. It's our world-

Alice interrupted Ted; her voice high-pitched with fear.

-Between Ted and you? You're Ted. Aren't you? You can't be Bob. I checked you. That's impossible-

Bob looked at Alice. Ted looked at Alice.

-We have two bodies. one mind. Two worlds to walk through by merely adjusting the channel-

Alice was gone. Her body in this world. Her mind suffering from a fracture.

Space is only a place to think in. It depends on your approach as to whether or not you can land. Thoughts like Alice's were not made for flying. Insistently the orange song. Ted sits dreaming behind the wheel of another world as the limo descends rapidly downhill.

HALF AN AURA

Spin this about on itself. Kid loved his son, IQ. Although only four he had a studious gaze. IQ knew something was missing from life because he was nervous. IQ barely knew his mother beyond the person that served him and his father at dawn and sunset. Going even further we could say that Kid wanted IQ to grow more than his mother wanted him to. She was afraid of the world's influence on her son. She mothered him to death until Kid interfered. IQ knew the difference. Kid borrowed lovers from time to time to replace the rhythm he had lost at home. Mother was just an image. An unfulfilled figure strolling in the kitchen, by the stove, hands in the refrigerator. Life is really unfortunate for some, maybe unfair but always certain, always complete.

Kid was in no hurry to go in the store. He was

smoking, good herb. The smoke rose out of his mouth into the air. He looked at IQ.

-Not right now. your mood ring is blue-

-It should be good as I feel. crawl over here and I'll let you out on my side-

-Ok-

IQ was very advanced for his age. He was already reading books but he was not very coordinated. A cause of concern to Kid whose family was very athletic. He had been a track star in high school and college when he met IQ's mother. Her family had the brains IQ inherited. Kid had recently taken up tennis. IQ was learning the piano. Crawling across the seat IQ got his feet tangled in the seat belt falling headlong out of the auto. Kid's reflexes were sharp.

-Gotcha-

IQ's eyes were as big as saucers.

-You ok? What the hell you doing. Damn you scared the crap out of me-

-I'm ok dad. my foot got tangled up in the seat belt-

-Ok but be careful IQ-

Some days however we can never be careful enough. Tragedy is coming no matter what we do. Get your rest, waste not a day in worry. You will have your name added to the list of characters already selected.

A

getaway car driven badly by some teenagers. Kid tried to move out of the way as the vehicle careened into them smashing IQ into the open door, knocking Kid to the ground. Kid could only see IQ's legs dangling in the air and the blood quietly falling to the ground like a soft rain.

-Is that a mood ring you got on?-

-What?-

-The ring on your finger, is that a mood ring?-

-Yeah. Why?

Kid was irritated by the little girl's question.

-It's black-

-Black?-

-Black. your ring is black-

The child's mother shushed the kid too late. Kid looked at his ring. It was black.

-He's on four miss-

She hurried to the elevator, then up, up and away. Kid was seated on a bench with his head down.

-You look beat Kid-

-Daphina it all happened so fast. I had just saved him from falling when this car just came out of nowhere and hit us. IQ was trapped in the door. Just that quick. Some young punks trying to make a getaway. I don't understand it we weren't doing anything wrong just going to the store.

-How is he?

-The doc said he will probably lose both his legs-

Daphina swayed and Kid helped her sit down. They waited for hours not saying a word. Finally, the doctor showed up and took them to a private room.

-The wounds were severe. We did the best we could but both legs will have to be removed. We need your permission-

Kid heard nothing else. Daphina handled the details. His mood dark and the feeling of emptiness covered him in shadows of betrayal. He put away the herbs and took up a life of drinking.

IQ took up life in a wheelchair. The once frail arms became muscled and his once dexterous fingers became thick from churning the wheels. True to his new form he became one of the most unusual humans to ever live. Seated now he applied himself to become freer. Studying long into the night the mechanics of the boats that rode on a cushion of air, he constructed a machine that he attached to a base he designed for his trunk. He hated the prosthetic legs of science. IQ's invention was so marvelous it completely revolutionized life for those of similar circumstance. It brought him millions and power. Kid died a happy man. Daphina died. For IQ life would not be a stumble. There were no friends with their false emotions of loving concern. IQ would never hear comments from those with all their parts.

-How are you today?

-Hope you feel better-

-Can I help you?

The

truth is that IQ was an awful person. IQ hated the world of his father and mother. He hated the world of the plumber and the barber. He hated the world of the speaker standing on his feet, on his own two legs. But most he hated the world of sex. Knees that could bend and plenty of meat. Naturally tender and naturally juicy, oh so sweet. IQ could only put in words between breaks for breath.

The

world had caused his accident and his dumb daddy hadn't paid attention. He remembered all the years when he used to feel a mess. So many eyes. Disturbing messages transmitted daily. He was afraid and could not go out at night. He was sixteen when he injured his first victim, giving the old lady a shove on the eleventh step. Later he said he had lost his balance on his prosthetic legs.

-I am very sorry, is she going to be all right?

IQ

enjoyed it more each time and he wasn't the one to be hurt. The millions he made from the bottom tuck air machine allowed him to travel freely. IQ was so sick he never knew only felt the need to respond in anger at the world for having made him so.

Alone

in his prison of detachment he looked out at the world through iron bars never understanding that what he did was wrong.

MORAL: the victims of tragedy sometimes sing her

favorite song

... seeing the world from the bottom up...

COLDEEN:

THEY SING SONGS ABOUT THIS

She

had a chain for childhood. Everybody, every day up to a frenzy, yelling about the absence of butter or bread or blankets to keep out the cold. The pain of generations and it truly hurts when you're one of the left out. The amber of the blues leans against the people in a house down the street and for several blocks around the corner that cast a shadow there.

Coldeen

came to each tomorrow without expectation ravaged constantly by her mother, the Chain. Walking without leaving footprints covering her trail with tales from Old Taylor or Jack Daniel's, bellowing without sound. Never a witness to gossip about the loud clangs of the Chain at a gallop. Sometimes she seems to caress, come in close to cut down the range between mixed feelings.

Feel

the Chain as she breathes. The pulsating sound of her rumble in her misery in each link tied to the master.

...evil in a bottle, evil on land, good only to the man with the right hands made for working off the walled...

They

sing songs about this, how everything wandered off and became tired. The morals of the people slipping to the floor. Who really came out to field a change. Not thieves or politicians but art, bodies to croon to and the Chain knew it, lived with it in secret. Her body trembling from its moisture like notes in a glass bottle. She would never escape from herself, the rooms smelling of emotion given in large doses to Coldeen.

Coldeen hugs herself. She closes her bedroom door to the lifeless things swirling in the room:

—drunk old bitch—

Next door on the second floor window practiced a horn in search of itself. Notes that made an exit from the bowl of eternity. The sound goes on still in search of itself, one day hoping to be fulfilled.

Some

of the nights were so long it seemed the stories of breathing in a neighborhood unable to tolerate the circumstances exuding from it were more than anyone could bear. A baby, Matti's to be specific, born and abandoned three days on fire escape metal steps and the time Jimmy's brother was killed for corn beef and beer. Fifteen of us sometimes standing around on the playground or just hanging out adding our own special tone to true stories and even outright lies. Talk about the "this could only happen to me" in-fighting. Little sluggers with no finesse and less training. Everybody's pants worn thin except the bail bondsman and hustlers, the funeral director and the preachers, they always gave thanks to the "In

God We Trust."

For

us it was the world we had handled. There was nothing beyond the window but a reflection of us drooping before the gates that led to the outer worlds. It took more than courage; it took the manhood of the years to get a hold of them gates and throw them open. God we want to see them and theirs without the lights always on bright. Why does it always take wisdom and endless heart?

And

yet, it was the things like the sound of his horn, hung out like a symbolic exit, the continuing echo of the slaves' cry for true freedom. Oh so sweet the sound. Holding on to that feeling that keeps us in the fight. Everywhere let them wait for the knockout the creator denies. We have been endowed with the hearts of giants.

It

takes more than water to survive life in the desert. There are many cells in the prison filled with magicians caught in the act. Next door the horn comes off the window. Pearl would be home soon dragging the dust from the street onto the porch where she would stop for a stomping, banging her feet on the old wood.

-don't bring none of that dirt in my house girl-

The chain told everybody that and then would disappear in the bottom of Jack Daniels. She had a lot of courage.

        oh yeah, Coldeen

        she was a Sarah

        a bone child

        and flesh of the sun

        guarded in the

        body of her adolescence

        but the men knew

        she had potential

—that man was looking for you again—

—well, he can come here if he want to but I still ain't going back to no school—

—just wanted you to know. gotta go, talk to ya when I get back—

—where you going Pearl—

—Candy having some dudes over—

—wake me up if I'm sleep so you can tell me about it, ok—

—Yeah, sure, be cool (at the door) oh the Chain rolled over when I came in—

—Maybe we ought to just hide them ol bottles—

—and she just get another and another, not on my money and not on my time. Look here Coldeen I gots to go. Don't want to keep them boys waiting. Stay up I should be back by ten or so—

Coldeen

listened to the sound of her sister's footsteps fade down the hall.

—think I'll change the color of this room. damn roaches, grease and dirt all over the walls. Momma need to quit all that drinking and clean this mess up. maybe we could wash'um first ..

-Coldeen? Coldeen? man named Mr. Sails here to see you (door opens) 'bout yo schooling. (heads back down the hall to the living room) –ain't I done tol you every morning to get yo behind outta here. Now you got this gentleman's coming up in my house. Put some clothes on and come in here-

Coldeen hugged herself

—lying bitch—

She opened the door.

2.

There

were countless numbers of people whose tools had helped hew the corners to keep her from falling off the edge into free thought. Constructing the invisible corridors that represented the distance of her mind and she became measurable because of their standards. But Coldeen's thoughts were full of questions that she couldn't answer like why children had no rights. She couldn't do anything without the Chain peering at her mind and it was the same with school and everywhere she went there were adults and rules. She was sick of rules and sick of being a kid.

Coldeen

was sure god had made everything and the world her mind lived in, lived on and the trees and ants, walking and creeping things.

Coldeen smiled to herself because these thoughts always brought to mind the Rev Sam and his loud raspy voice pouring out the waters of love of god. She had to leave church one day because he suddenly appeared funny to her all dressed up in a costume and screaming in front of an audience giving him amens and hallelujahs. This thought frightened her later. She was beginning to interpret life.

Deep

inside of her was laughter but it was held up by the invisible boundaries society had placed there since her memory realized this world. She hadn't really laughed in three or four years, since the day in church after her sister Bobbie left. Bobbie was silly and skinny as could be. She would laugh at almost anything. There was a man that worked at the corner store, a white man and he had the smallest mouth Bobbie said she had ever seen. Bobbie was fourteen then. Once upon a time she said she was in the store and he was trying to drink a bottle of pop. One of those big quarter pops and somehow it got stuck in his mouth. She said she laughed so hard she almost peed on herself and then the next day she was gone, runaway.

That

left Coldeen on the edge. The place where all the

thoughts of men had collected and turned into granite, stone, a wall trying to advance into the next day. Coldeen felt like she was in a teepee just outside of the mental landscape men had created and she was a tribe of one.

3.

—ain't seen her in five or six weeks. yeah we friends but I don't go see her cause her momma act funny-

—no she never came to class—

—she came once but then she left. she was

daydreaming and I think I embarrassed her—

—look as far as I'm concerned none of them have to come. they can all stay home or wherever they go—

—we don't know why Coldeen quit coming to school—

Nothing

is promised but everything is fulfilled. This kind of war is never over. All my life at the beginning, up to the threshold like magazine lips you pass your imagination through.

I'm

like you Coldeen, they never really knew where I was at. Somehow I emerged on the other side even though I had shared the same sun on a similar street on a bed on Lily and she was fine and I loved her.

Coldeen

probably has been made to serve the phonies and the oldies. Music saved me maybe hers will be biscuits served by a sincere hand if it's not too late.

When

I meet them though they're always different from what I hope. Each of their little faces peeping through a hole they've made to see the world.

Some

of the holes not big enough to put their heads through only a hand or a foot or a slot they can see through but never really seeing enough of the world to make a difference. Drifting back into the world of shadows hollowed out by shadow figures slowly sinking deeper and deeper into prisons occupied by other visitors strolling to the music of the lost soldiers of alcohol or prison or loneliness or poverty. Some of them came armed for revolution to overcome the smoke of awe flying far above their heads. Their senses frightened into a continual state of dullness and inactivity. They go through this life roped.

Mr. Sails noticed that the quiet around Coldeen sank through the floor. She was housed with an occupant that was impossible.

—this here's my baby gurl, Mary Coldeen Johnson—

—how do you do—

—hi—

—Jimmy take Pearl's baby in the otha room so's

Mr. Sails and we in here can hear. Now sir yes (motioned him to a chair). Now Mary Coldeen Johnson you tells Mr. Sails how I tries to get you outta here. Every morning I tells her to get up. Just like I tells the rest of them but I tell you sir right now, that she just don't listen. She goes outta here big as day sometimes and damn near an hour later she right back again. Now sir I tells you I am sick to death with running back and forth to that school 'bout this here gurl. Now Mary Coldeen Johnson you tell him 'bout this and what I've tried to do for you. I got to finish my cooking—

-Well, Mrs. Johnson—

—her daddy's name was Johnson, my name is Hatia Gealiha. Ms. g-a-le-ha—

—Excuse me Ms. Gealiha. I was hoping on this first visit that I could meet and talk with the family—

—ain't no need for that. everybody round here knows how Mary Coldeen Johnson is. just the otha day her and Pearl was argumenting cause Mary don't help keep that room of theirs clean and picked up—

—aw momma that ain't what we was talking about. see you always get things wrong—

—now gurl don't you be telling me I ain't heard what I heard. you trying to make somebody think I'm crazy. I was sitting right ova there on that couch looking out that window.

—is there much family feuding. I mean between your children?—

—now sir I'll tell you right now, you see Mary wants to be like her sister. Fast. Grownup. well, her sister, Bobbie's her name, she run west, live on a farm or something. wrote me one letter in three years. ain't seen her face on tv or newspapers, ain't heard her sing no songs, nothing. I tries to tell Mary about schooling but she just go humph and fold her arms—

Coldeen hugged herself. She watched the man's eyes looking at her feet. Dirty on the bottom from walking barefoot. She put them down flat on the floor. She saw his eyes take in her body more than once. The Chain's body. The walls of the house. Studying the room as if he were taking pictures. Click-Jimmy's smelly tennis shoes by the door. Click-the tv running errantly. Click-the roach making his way down the hall. Click-a fly on the baby's bottle. Click-the dog wandering in wagging his tail.

—go outside dog, Jimmy come get this dog—

The Chain's voice snapped Coldeen's head back to the moment. Mr. Sails was preparing to leave.

—I'm sure we can work something out. So we'll see you in school tomorrow at eight—

—Yeah—

—now you heard this gentleman and you know you know what we got to do so we get past this thing. I don't wants no more gentleman's coming up here from the school cause of you and your unappearance!

Pearl

was stomping her feet as Mr. Sails was exiting. He

hesitated for just a moment while Pearl went through her ritual. Stomping and stomping the world's plagues from the soles of her shoes.

Mr. Sails

slowed the auto at the corner and then away.

Up ahead two girls were fighting and some kids in a circle were choosing sides. He slowed long enough to hear three different kids say "kick her muthafucking ass." Some adults were coming down the street so he pulled off. Sails watched in the rear view. The angry crowd had gotten larger as more adults showed up. All he could see now were hands jerking in the air and necks rocking. He drove past a broken old man with little flesh on his skeleton burning under the sun. His hands stuffed in the pockets of a long coat. A drama of people of color with white hands controlling the strings of black puppets cooking over a low fire.

Sails

lost sight of the crowd on a right curve. Sails found himself at home with Omi, her soft lips giving his dry mouth much-needed moisture.

So

the ritual of life continues its juggling act amazing to us all. Is tomorrow just another day I have yet to use or is there something spectacular waiting just around the bend.

NEPTUNE'S SERVANT

I only just this moment came in from the rains. God today was a day of work. See here my boots and clothing caked in mud. Today we lifted and hauled and shooed flies away. Then the rain, a little and then the sun. Kept things so confused we nearly missed lunch. They say I'm not much on size but I'm Neptune's servant. You didn't know me then heh? Yes, I'm Neptune's servant—

I suppose you haven't heard what happened to Tikko. The man he worked for was named Crackus and he was the foreman for a lumber business up on the north mountain. His men worked a double shift for almost two weeks. Tikko was the first one of us in more than a generation to reach the position of boss. Crackus had made him foreman of a large section of the mountain and he also oversaw bringing the wood down. Nobody was better in the Tokano Pass River than Tikko. He was one of the most natural woodsmen any of us had ever seen. Even as a kid he was a man among boys, over six feet tall, sinewy and swift. He told me one time he feel the heartbeat of the trees, felt their breathing stop as they collided violently with the earth. Many nights he could be found asleep on the mountain's side lying next to one of the giant trees he fought to protect from Crackus' blazing saws. They had had more than one violent confrontation. Crackus told him he was a madman.

These

trees feed our families, make wood for ships to go sailing off this god forsaken island to bring us fish. You and I know on this one hundred mile island there are not enough animals to feed all the people. without the ships we would have no meat. You can't protect these trees forever. If it weren't for the crazy notions of our ancestors I would have cut them down years ago.

You

know it always surprises people when you discover the dark side of someone and Tikko had one. He was secretly a greedy man and very selfish although that is not the face he presented to the world. Now, I figured Tikko would put in his time, make his money and retire fat and happy and spend his time sailing which he said was his real love. it seems as though Crackus had discovered a vein of gold in one of the many caves on the south mountain which was mostly barren from a volcanic explosion many years ago. The forest was slowly returning but the wood was still too virgin for logging. It was said Tikko had come upon Crackus one night creeping up the mountain and had followed him. Tikko went into the cave after Crackus had left and saw with his own two eyes what Crackus was trying to keep secret. Crackus found chips of stone left by someone working his mine and footprints. He decided to find out who was stealing from him. One night a big storm struck the island and Tikko figured this would be a good time to make his way back to the cave and take as much gold as possible. The storm lasted through the night and Tikko weary from the work had fallen asleep. Crackus discovered him there and the two men had a violent fight with knives. The blood of Tikko splattered on his sacks of stolen gold. Crackus hauled him back to town and made a lie of it to keep his gold a secret.

I

was on the mountain myself that morning and witnessed what really happened. Crackus had taken Tikko to that mountain and knifed him. I felt for Tikko because his greed probably would have gotten him killed anyway. It was a bad thing because so many of our people were forced into lives of thievery and riffraff. Crackus presented himself like a hero at our expense and was accepted as such. Yes I am Neptune's servant and that Crackus is dead.

My

family goes back more than eleven generations. Since we came into this world we've seen both sides of things. One of my ancestors had long elegant fingers and was married to a wealthy man. Her grandson squandered the family fortune, tricked by the tribe of Crackus's ancestors. When he was born he was given the seal of Pluto which was supposed to be an amulet given an ancestor by some forgotten king. I have worked since I was fourteen with one goal in mind; to be what my family once was.

Yes

I am Neptune's servant and I have only recently come in from the rain. I have taken many steps with one step. Crackus sleeps for the lie he told and what is yellow and cold sleeps with me tonight. For myself and my people I have changed the position of the world and look forward to the day when my children's children will ask other men to pay.

I

am Neptune's servant and I have only recently come in from the rain. It's been a long day and I am tired. Tomorrow, maybe tomorrow will bring the light of the southwest stars and reveal the relationship of mysteries still uncovered.

...it's who you keep that's important...

THE GRUMBLERS

The

men of power sat around the large oak lunch table. The dark purple curtains with their gold trimmings and the Persian rugs overtly displayed the wealth permeating the club's atmosphere.

—well, son how is things over at that company of yours, going pretty good from what we have seen—

—AJ things are all quiet now but for a year or so things were a little hairy. I mean production was good; in fact we were growing at a pretty good clip—

The

talking at the table faded into the Persian rugs. Some of the men at the tables lowered their brows with rapt interest.

—what do you mean you took care of your hairy problems Phillip?—

—I'm sure I don't have to tell you about how some employees can be a nightmare. Grumbling at every change as if the world was coming to an end, stirring up trouble—

—I see. Tell me Philip what did you do, get rid of all of your grumblers?—

The concern of the men of power turned to smiles at this suggestion.

—Yes, I did, each and every one of them. I

got some of my best employees to identify all the troublemakers and fired them all—

The men of power's faces let out an audible scream.

-what did he say-

-no, I don't believe it-

-ah, Phillip tell me you didn't let each and everyone of your grumblers get away?-

—yes. why isn't that what all of you do. I heard you talk about how you got rid of this rotten apple or the girl who was a bad egg—

—thieves or the violent ones or the ones who don't come to work of course but grumblers, tell him AJ not the grumblers, maybe one or two to keep the chains in place but all the grumblers along with the rest of the basket of bad employee's never—

—that's right, isn't it AJ. all of us know the value of grumblers. tell me Phillip how's your production now—

—yeah, now that things are so quiet how are things going?-

—I don't know, it's kinda weird. Everything's so quiet I don't know what's going on. Baltimore, the guy that was always coming by my office with tidbits of information hasn't said a word to me in over a week. I haven't seen a falloff in production but now that I think of it when I walk the floor something is missing-

-take it from me Phillip, AJ has been down that road. When I took over the business from my father one of the first things I did was to get rid of all the grumblers along with the rest of the bums. The old man came to me when he found out what I had done and asked me what in the hell did I think I was doing firing Beatrice. I told him she was a grumbler and always criticized the company, complained loud and long to everybody that would listen. And you know what he said to me Phillip, he said so what. I said so what. He said yes so what and then he gave me the greatest management tool he ever gave me. He said AJ without the grumblers there is no way for executives like us to ever hear what's really going on. A job is like a community and the grumblers keep everything going. Do you know that some people come to work just to grumble; you know complain about this or that. Others also listen or talk with the grumblers and make decisions that affect how work is going. Your man Baltimore feels less effective and is afraid now that he has nothing to report to you his job may be in jeopardy. In fact since you fired all the hard cases the only things you've got left now are the *do-gooders, snitches, and brown-nosers*. A few regulars that swing left or right depending on the issue but now since there are no grumblers there are no issues and worst of all there is now no social fabric, no gossip and no comedians because the people you've got left are mainly timid, afraid of the boss types not good fodder for those that can lead. Among some of those grumblers was a boss just waiting to emerge. You know the guy or girl that can take it on the chin and give as good as they get, men and women not afraid to speak their minds. Not all grumblers are grumblers some are supervisors and they have to be leaders to command the respect of their peers, come from their ranks to show that one of them can rise up the ranks. Phillip if you don't correct this and soon you're gonna have worms in your soup. You're killing your own community.

All the men of power of nodded their heads in agreement.

The

next day Phillip walked through the shop.

AJ was right as he tried to engage the eyes of his employees they avoided his gaze and greeted him with timid hellos as if he were carrying a hatchet.

Even Terry who was always laughing was looking serious. Later that day Irene in personnel called him and told him that four employees resigned.

-Did they tell you why they were leaving-?

-Well, from what I can gather the employees are unhappy, afraid that since you were willing to get rid of the hard cases that everybody's job was at risk-

-Thank you Irene. I want you to call that girl Malicia and tell her to report to work tomorrow if she hasn't found a job yet-

-sir didn't you fire her last week for insubordination-?

-yes but I found out something I didn't know, now call her and let me know what she says—

Phillip pressed his hands against his throbbing head decided to call AJ.

—AJ? Phillip. I had four people quit today after I toured the plant. Yes, no one looked me in the eye. Well, I realize now that it was a mistake. I asked my HR person to call back one of the ladies I fired last week. Yes, two or three more. Ok and I'll talk to the others to see if I can get them to stay. Yes, I understand this is the worms you were talking about. Ok AJ thanks, I'll call you back in a few days—

The

men of power were all anxious to see Phillip. AJ had told them about the worms. News like this could spread. Phillip came into the hall.

-Well, what's happening Phillip—

—AJ I have to tell you it's amazing. As soon as Malicia got back to work she started complaining. Baltimore told me the whole thing. She shouldn't have been fired in the first place. She should have gotten a raise. and because of her Randy, Cross, Cuphill and Ms. Hingiss all got their jobs back but she did admit how much she missed the gang at work and how bored she was because she wasn't working and how everybody better get back to work before they get her fired and maybe this time she won't get her job back-

A

servant coming into the dining area thought he was seeing things. The men of power were leaping about and whooping and hollering as if they all had just helped Phillip score a touchdown.

—Bring wine man, wine and plenty of it, we're celebrating a victory of immeasurable proportions—

None of the men of power left the club sober that night and the whole event was talked about for weeks.

...yes, some people are born special...

BALIN

—mother look at his feet—

--my god, we thought this thing had passed us by, now here it is again. he even has the purple lock of his great great uncle—

The

doctor wrote in his notes:

height-baby boy twenty-two inches long.

weight-seven pounds

abnormalities-six toes and an Achilles heel appendage in the shape of a small fleshy fin.

The nurse handed the mother a sheet of paper.

—please write the name of your child here-

The mother, Francona wrote Balin Makets. He was the last child born to Francona, the fifth of five brothers and two sisters, Ma'kaly and Ta'kely, the twins.

—Balin take out the trash—

—Balin sweep the floor—

—Balin wash the dishes—

—Balin let's go fishing—

That would be his sister Ma'kaly. She didn't really care so much for fishing she just liked walking in the woods and she loved water especially the river Slow. That's what they called it because the water barely moved or at least that's what it seemed like.

One day Balin put a toy boat in the water, gave it a little push and they watched as the boat moved slowly out into the middle of the river and just sat there. They came back the next day and the boat had only went a few feet downstream. The bend in the river was no more than fifty steps from their favorite spot and it took the toy boat a whole week to get there. Even the rain could not speed up the river. It was like the town it ran behind. Nothing moved fast in the town of Meander, in fact that's how the town got its name.

That

is until Balin was born. He was quick, unusually quick. He learned to walk by the time he was seven months old and was talking when he was one. He even grew quickly especially his feet. He could outrun and outjump and outswim his brothers and everybody else in the town. His father, Master Buckly Makets paid little attention to his family. He was a truck driver and came home once a month for a couple days and then headed out again.

—nine mouths to feed don't leave a man much time for sitting around being useless-

When the oldest boy, Pag, was old enough he took him on the road to help drive the big rig.

—Makee (Ma'kaly) what you gone do when you grow up?-

—don't know, but I ain't sticking around here and grow old with a bunch of kids like ma. I'm leaving here as soon as I turn eighteen-

—Where you going-

—don't know, why you always asking me about being grown—

—cause—

—cause what. why you always in such a hurry—

—I ain't in no hurry I just want to get where I'm going that's all—

—boy you ain't even twelve yet and I just turned

fourteen. It's that coach ain't it, the one from that school that saw you running after that train—

—aw that wasn't nothing that train had just started to move—

—yeah but that coach told momma he ain't never seen no kid run like that—

Coach Cutt

thought he was seeing things. It was just after sundown when Balin came out of nowhere and chased down the train jumping onto the last car.

—just like a baby deer—

That's what he told momma that night when he followed Balin home.

—M'am, you and your husband should bring that boy of yours around so we can take a better look at him. Your son has some unusual athletic ability—

Francona's

fears were aroused. The world would treat him like a freak when they discovered he has six toes and a fleshy fin on his Achilles heel. His great great uncle was treated that way until the day he died.

—The doctors said they could operate and remove the extra toe-

—Francona they also said that fooling with that Achilles fin thing could make him a cripple-

—Buckly maybe we could get another opinion, Dr. Laten is just a country doctor—

—good enough for me. good enough to see you through the birthing of all these kids and all of them is healthy. let it alone Francona, the boy is born just the way god wanted it and we shouldn't ought to fool with what god made—

Balin

started high school over at the new county high school, Meander County High. One day the coach saw him and asked him to come out for the track team.

—you know I never forgot what I saw you do that night chasing that train. Do you still chase the trains—

—No Coach Cutt, that's kid stuff. I'm going to be a veterinarian like my sister. I go with her sometimes and help with the animals and stuff—

—Anybody in your family ever play sports-

—nope, I mean we swim and play games but no nobody ever played for a team or nothing. My dad said that was a useless waste of good time. besides ain't no guarantees you gone be successful, then what you got. My dad always raised us to get a trade or something or drive trucks like he does—

—well, you're right there ain't no guarantees in sports, you might even get hurt or something but then there are no guarantees about anything in life. if you change your mind come see me in the spring. I think you got something special. You just need to give us a chance to see exactly what you got-

—ok coach, we'll see—

The

winter that year was hard. It acted as though it didn't want spring to come. Kept coming back with an extra cold wind from the north. Finally the sun broke the icy grip of winter.

Slow took a little longer to thaw. Balin ran his mind over what the coach had said. There was not a boy in the county that could beat him running but his extra toe made it hard for him to get shoes and his feet hurt. Most of the time when he ran he did it in private so he could take his shoes off and free his feet from the binds of tape and leather.

Spring

busted out and decorated herself in a splash of colors and warm breezes.

—mom, I think I'm going to try out for the track team—

—did you talk to your father?-

—sorta. he said he ain't buying me no shoes for that nonsense. my regular shoes cost too much as it is—

Francona's mind was stuck on the image of seeing her soon being ridiculed and laughed at, a freak with a winged Achilles heel. Buckly was right there was no way they could afford to buy the special shoes he would need.

—I like running mom. I like jumping too—

Coach Cutt

was surprised to see Balin the day he came out to watch the team practice. They were already in the second week and he had given up on trying to convince the boy.

—Well, Balin, I didn't think you was interested. Do you have shoes—

Inspecting the boy's feet he noticed that they were wider than most boys' feet his size. Balin was now nearly six feet two and fifteen years old.

—what size shoe you wear, looks like a thirteen but your feet are a little wide. are you flat footed?

—no—

—alright, go in the locker room and see the trainer. he'll get you fixed up and hurry we're almost halfway through training today. We got a big meet coming up next week and I'd like to see what you can do against some real competition.—

—coach told me to see you about some shoes—

—ok son, sit down over there let's get you measured up—

Balin took off his shoes and socks and the trainer's eyes bugged when he saw the six toes.

—what you got there boy an extra toe? does the coach know about this?—

Balin shook his head.

—size thirteen but we ain't got nothing wide enough to fit you. I'll have to get the coach-

A

few minutes later both men returned. The look on the coach's face spoke without him saying any words.

—put your foot out. what's that tape around your heels for, you hurt your heels?

Balin removed the tape and the fleshy fin popped out. Both men took a step backward as if the fins were an animal with teeth set to attack them.

—what the hell is this. you come out of the sea or something?

—no. I was born this way—

—what you think coach—

—I don't know what to think. I ain't never seen nothing like this before. Son you better just go on home while we try to figure this out—

Francona

could not hide her tears. It was what she had feared. He was a freak to the world. She should never have let him try out for the team, should have done everything in her power to discourage it. They could hide the purple lock with dye but his feet and the fin could not be hidden from view unless bound with tape and surrounded with leather. Big wide feet were one thing, six toes and a fin were something different.

A

week went by and the big meet came and went. Balin heard nothing from Coach Cutt and Master Buckly Makets was embarrassed as all get out.

—boy what did I tell you. Sports ain't for you. They don't want you. Can't you see that. By now it's all over the county, you got six toes and a fin on your ankles. You know anybody else that's got that? Only you and your dead uncle, nobody else. And they treated him like a freak all his life-

One

day Coach Cutt sent the trainer to get Balin. Balin

could barely contain his excitement. Despite everything he now knew that he wanted to run and jump.

—I got some shoes for you. these are specially made, designed to cover that thing on your ankles and extra wide. now they may slow you down a little because they weigh a few more ounces than regular track shoes. if they fit you'll need another pair designed for jumping. let's head out to the track and try them out.—

Word had indeed got out about Balin's unusual appendages and some of the boys on the team wore some silly grins on their faces.

—wipe them smiles off your faces—

Coach Cutt was all business.

—all right you four on the track. I want you to run a hundred yard dash and not too fast. I don't want anybody pulling any muscles or anything. Balin join them. on your mark, get set . . . go.

It

was the wind that got into Balin as he sailed across the cinder track. Coach Cutt never forgot that first day. Balin was a thing of beauty as he raced around the track ahead of the pursuing pack. One hundred yards, two hundred yards, three hundred yards and finally the whole quarter mile. Balin didn't just run he sailed, running with the wind, through it to the finish. Nobody could beat him. His smile spreading across his face as he released the energy of his body in each step.

The

town of Meander had a track star. A kid born to run. News spread quickly. The first time anything ever moved fast in the hundred year history of the town.

Meander High won every meet they entered and then it was time for the state meet in the city of Regina.

The

feet of Balin had taken a terrible pounding. The doctors had explained to Coach Cutt that Balin's bones were fragile, thinner than most. It was first noticed at a meet in Meckly that Balin's time was slower although he won the race. The trend continued and by the race in Athens two weeks before the state meet he had lost his first race, finishing third and in extreme pain. The doctor's conclusion was confirmed by the swelling in his feet and the pain in his hips from the piston action of his knees.

—what should I do coach—

--go home and rest son. the doctors said that's the only thing to do—

By the time the big state meet came Balin could barely run at all.

—coach I can still jump. Barnett and the others can hold their own on the track. I can win the high jump and we can win the meet-

—I don't know Balin. you got to use your ankles and toes to push off—

—I know coach but I've been going over in my mind a way to do it so I can jump—

—I don't know—

-coach, if what the doctors say is true this will probably be my last meet anyway. I won't be able to do anything like running or jumping again. My family has never had anybody get this kind of attention except my great great uncle and they thought he was a freak because he also had six toes and fins on his ankles. I want this chance—

—but it could ruin you, make you a cripple—

—people already think I'm some kind of freak. if I'm not going to be able to do this again I want this one last opportunity—

—ok son but if I see you can't make it I'm pulling you, understand?   you got to clear six feet to qualify, can you do that?

-yes, but I'm going to sit out the rest of the jumps

 until the last one-

—but that'll mean you will only have one jump to win—

—I'll only need one—

It

was a day that would go down in sports lore.

Balin

cleared the six feet and then passed on the next three rounds receiving two penalties against him for not jumping. The bar was at seven feet. Only Mark Wiscost was left and he cleared the seven feet with two misses and one left. Balin approached the bar and requested it be raised to seven three. The announcement was made on the stadium loudspeakers and a roar went up from the crowd.

Francona and Buckly and Balin's brothers and sisters cheered loudly.

Balin

went over in his mind what he needed to do to clear the bar. He got the idea from watching gymnastics. He noticed how high the tumblers got when they made their flips. He counted his steps and knew he would need to be about eight feet from the bar to do the first flip that would propel him into a second flip from which he would somersault in midair over the bar. He decided the best way to do this was to remove his shoes and go barefoot. He needed all the power his toes could deliver.

The

crowd watched in disbelief as Balin ran with his beautiful stride and then suddenly somersaulted on his hands twice into a flip like a gymnast landing on his feet and immediately pushing off with all of his might into a tight ball somersaulting through the air flipping himself over the bar and landing on his feet on the other side of the bar.

Balin

took a deep breath and began running with all his might and somersaulted on his hands twice turning himself and landing on his feet and immediately   exploding into a somersaulting flip. He saw the bar underneath him as he sailed into the still air flipping himself over it and landed on his feet. For a few seconds he heard nothing but the sound of his breathing because he had been concentrating so hard. When the sound struck the stadium it came across like a gale. Coach Cutt had him in his arms. Several photographers that had taken pictures were shaking their heads.

Mark Wiscost didn't even attempt to make the jump and Meander County High School was state champs for the first and only time.

Coach Cutt

smiled at the trophy in the main hall of the school along with the historic photo of Balin's flip, a now famous style added to high jumping techniques.

The

newspapers lined the floor and wall of the Maket household. The photos of Balin's flip were everywhere. It was the first time anybody had ever applied the somersaulting techniques of gymnastics to high jumping. Everyone said it was fantastic and no one made any comments about Balin's six toes or the fleshy fin. Most just said it was extraordinary and very remarkable. The sequence of photos and the tv cameras captured his heroics for all time.

...it only comes once a year and then...

THE RED COAT

If

I were going to tell you a good story I wouldn't begin by telling you that Dix had four brothers and four sisters or that he was the oldest child of Dixan and Fray Evening. No, I wouldn't tell you about a time in the thirties when America was in the bowels of a deep depression and many of her people stood in soup lines. I would get right to the point and tell you two things. First there is nothing more special than young love and second there is hardly anything more satisfying than seeing a boy becoming a man. This is the story of Dix and Oma.

-boy where you been disappearing to every day-

-I been working-

-you take your brother with you-

-they said he was too young-

-Fray pass me them potatoes. You kids can only have a half a liver apiece, except you Dix. You the oldest, me and you passing on meat tonight—

—again—

-what you say boy. you got potatoes and greens with tomatoes, bread and a slice of cheese, same as me. you don't hear me complaining do you—

There

were no other words possible to come from Dix only that same look he had two days ago when the family had breakfast of sausage and eggs and grits only he and his dad had cheese.

-I'm tired of this shit—

-boy are you saying something under your breath. I know damn well you ain't mumbling at my dinner table—

Dixan

was a hard man. Like most of the black men that returned home from the first World War he had fled the south for the north.

-if I had stayed in Georgia I would've killed me a white man for sure—

That's all he said and many of the black men that migrated to Cleveland's lower Eastside felt the same way. Farming and slaving were over.

-I'm a man and I'm raising my boys to be men and girls to be women. Ain't gone be kissing no white man's ass and working for Miss Anne-

Fray

was a woman of her time. She had never worked a job. Her duties were in the house and with nine kids that was more than a full load. Now if you want me to I could tell you about wash days when her and the girls would load up the machine, the scrub board, and wash clothes all day and hang them out to dry. The whole neighborhood and all the backyards full of clothes sailing back and forth on a summer breeze.

The

first time Dix saw Oma she was hanging clothes. Well, actually she was chasing a flying pillow case, blue I was told. The pillowcase landed right at his feet. He looked into her brown eyes and that was it.

-well, are you gone just stand there staring or are you going to hand me my laundry-

Dix

said later he didn't remember what he said all he could remember was the way she smiled at him and he loved it. He did talk about her legs and the way she walked and he did say she turned around and waved goodbye to him before she turned the corner at the back of her house and went into the backyard. He remembered finding all kinds of reasons to walk down his street, cross the street and go down one block, turn left onto her street and walk slowly past her house. He was in some kind of fog.

-boy what's wrong with you your eyes been looking funny like you done been some place. you ain't using none of that dope I hear some folks been fooling with. pass me some more of them potatoes and give that boy some meat tonight—

-ain't nothing wrong with him daddy except some girl name Oma he been dreaming about-

-Oma? what kind of name is that-

-shut up Lizy, you need to mind your own business, you and that Roy sneaking around behind the garage the other day-

-both of yaw shut up. Dammit yaw the oldest and still fussing like little kids-

-he started it the other day. he didn't have no right chasing Roy out the yard. hit that boy with a stone in the head-

-yeah and I'd'a done more than that if I had got my hands on him-

-I still got my strap hanging over there. I done tol' you before no boys round here and you mister man better follow my advice or some girl's father or brothers gone want a piece of your ass-

I

guess some things are just meant to be. When school started you already know what happened next. Yup, they had two classes together, English and math and in math he was two seats away from her. It took a few weeks but finally they got together at a school dance. I'm not going to bore you with the details there are plenty of romance novels and movies and poems for that. All I want you to do right now is remember the first time you really fell in love with someone. How sometimes it's hard to talk and other times the words are coming so fast you can't slow them down. Taking the long way home and the inevitable first time you touch each other's skin and feel the heat of the exchange of your breath and the sweetness of lips when first they induce you into intimacy. Passion when you're young is a wild bucking stallion that lifts its skirts releasing the first surprise of early moisture and wet pants.

Unfortunately

no story is really interesting until something happens. Without the kick of drama it's just another uneventful day. Trying to grow into a man is a difficult thing. There are no rites of passages like killing a wild beast or walking hot coals. In

America a man becomes a man when he becomes a man. It is sort of like being responsible for a family but it's also about how one acts, carries himself. I mean, yeah you got be tough so other men will respect you but then you got to have a gentle side so you can attract girls and an even gentler side for little kids and old people. And you got to sacrifice, take less so others can have more or at least enough. Dix looked at the men in his neighborhood. Sometimes when he and Oma would walk through the neighborhood or down one of the two main streets, Central or Cedar, they would talk about what they wanted to do with their lives when they were grown.

-I don't know Dix I love tap dancing but I can't make any money here I'd have to go to New York or Chicago. What about you?

-well I sure can't make any money running track. I love art and sometimes when I'm downtown I look at the buildings and say to myself, heck I can design a better building than that or cars, I mean I think they're too long. I like the older ones better-

-me too. although I do like that new Packard-

-not me, I've always liked Cadillacs, classiest car on the road-

-so are you saying you want to be an architect or something—

-I don't know about that you got to have good math skills for that. I thought about drafting but I don't have money for that. you got to go to college for that-

-well, what about a scholarship for track-

-yeah, that's a possibility but then I would have to leave Cleveland, go away downstate to Ohio State or some other school-

-I saw your picture in the paper last year. you won state in the half mile, set a record-

-what! you mean you knew who I was that day in front of your house-

-of course silly boy-

-let's take the bus downtown. it's Sunday. I want to

show you something-

-all the way downtown—

-yeah, I don't feel like going to the movies today—

-oh really-

-really, you're not the only one who can withhold information-

When

they got downtown that day they went immediately to a clothing store called Rosenthals. A very expensive clothier. In the window he showed her the red coat of her dreams. Black fox fur on the collar and the end of the sleeves and side pockets, full length with four large black buttons.

-it's beautiful Dix-

-it's yours-

-mine-

-yours. well, in sixty days it will be. got to have it out of layaway before Christmas-

-if it's for Christmas why are you telling me now-

-so you'll know how much I love you, besides the sales lady said it has to be tried on first because they run small. you remember I had to come downtown with my mother last week to go to the farmers market. well, she came over here doing her usual window shopping and that's when I saw it. I got her to pretend I was going to buy one for her and when she tried the coat on in her size it was too small. that's when I found out the coat has to be tried on and if I got the wrong size they don't exchange them because they sew your name inside the coat.

-oh Dix I love you. when can I try it on—

-I already got your name on file and made the first deposit. all you got to do is come in get fitted and I'll take care of the rest-

-you know what you really think you slick don't you. I'm still not giving you none. momma told me to watch you boys, especially handsome ones like you, get a girl's heart all fluttery and then next thing you know you pregnant and he gone-

-Oma my daddy is always talking about making a man out of me. what you think I'm doing. I ain't up to nothing just trying to show my girl that she made the right choice. I'm not going to live like my father. I'm going to have my own house, my own car, all my kids gone have meat on their plates and my woman is gone be just as clean as I am. I'm gone live my life like the way I think a man should live-

-and how is that mister man-

-damn woman you sound like my daddy. that's what he calls me when he says I get too full of myself-

-does he now. ok mister man if you can do all that like what you say I just might come along for the ride-

-I already got you locked in that's why you ain't going to no New York and be no tap dancer. This our stop let's get off this bus or we'll have to walk two blocks back-

-wait a minute, what you mean I can't go to no

New York and tap. I love tap dancing-

-yeah, but you been tap dancing on my heart since the day I saw you-

and I don't intend to stop-

You

know the thing about stories that makes them interesting is when they get interesting. Sometimes intrigue works well you know like a murder mystery but I like the stories that get into life. You can't imagine how a simple thing like buying your girlfriend an expensive red coat can cause such a commotion. Maybe you can when you consider the circumstances. Dix is seventeen. it is October 1941. there is a war in Europe. Dixan Evening is working in a foundry making just enough to keep his family fed and a roof over there heads. Sometimes his thoughts wandered back to 1919 when he left the family farm in Georgia. Seven hundred acres that belonged to him and his brothers, passed down after his daddy died.

-boy you just become what you become. If you ain't got farming in you the land will break you before the white man get a chance too, believe that-

That's

what his father Clear Evening had told them. Farming is in the blood because the land is in the blood.

-if you ain't got no land to build on you ain't got nothing. you just running around squatting on some other man's place. Now you tell me what kind of man want to run around squatting on another mans place. I got a house here and I got plenty to eat. I kills my own hogs and slaughters my beef, I got chickens and fields full of beans and corn and all kinds of vegetables. I got a house with two fireplaces and I don't owe no man nothing. I'll be damn if I'm gone follow anybody up north to live on another man's land and pay him a fee for squatting. One day the white man gone get tired of mistreating folks or folks gone get tired of his mess and everybody gone together and whup the shit out of white folks. I ain't never been able to understand why they so sick and the sad thing about it everybody in the world knows it but him. Killing and lynching folks. wonder how they feel if somebody had a picnic while they asses got strung up for being white-

Now the one real problem that the Evening men had was drinking. And Dixan remembered how his daddy would get in his *corn* likker and talk about white folks and black folks and how some Indian used to work for his daddy and taught him how to grow corn and make popcorn and how to make leather.

It seems like the stories keep going back into time in one life only to come back again in the life of one of the kids.

-boy you come up a little short on your rent ain't you-

-I had to buy me a pair of shoes and I needed another shirt-

-shoes and a shirt. well, where they at, I ain't seen 'um yet-

Sometimes

Dixan liked to play with people's minds, especially if he thought they might be lying. He had told Fray the other night that Dix was up to something.

-probably that Oma. going to the movies and taking her out to eat-

-Dixan leave that boy alone. you said you wanted our kids to have a different life than me and you. you been working regular hours now for the last year, you making more money than you ever did. he works hard at that laundry, pressing clothes and delivering-

-yeah but Fray there's a war in Europe. this ain't the right time for all that kinda stuff. you know these white folks over here is itching to get in this war. I seen what happened in the last one and they wouldn't even let us hardly fight. never seen so much blood and destruction. whole cities full of streets with buildings torn apart. Fray you ever wonder if we should have ever left the south, the farm. Sometimes I think about what my daddy said about being a squatter, paying rent on another man's land. Not having meat enough for everybody-

-after coming back from that war could you have really stayed. no we sacrificed a lot but you probably would have wound up killing some man mean as you are-

-mean. I ain't mean-

-Dixan you just like your daddy. you don't like the word no, won't take a step back for anybody and won't allow any man, not even Reverend Holman to touch my hand-

-that son of a bitch can go to hell. him and all them preachers lying to people week after week-

-no, we ain't going there tonight, goodnight-

-I seen him and Miss Oma downtown-

-I didn't ask for your mouth to get in this did I Lizy. Now you want to tell me what's going on mister man-

-ain't nothing going on. I put the shoes in the lay away and the shirts hanging up in the closet.-

-boy! yeah you, the youngest go get me that shirt-

-nice shirt. white with that new collar. what you doing boy going dancing under the light while these here in this house may get cut off. you know I don't understand you. every time I think you coming into manhood you slip back a few years-

Some things are just inevitable. We've all been through this one way or another. A young man who's had enough of some crazed daddy. One day you just simply crack up with tears flowing and rebellion making its way out your soul and you raise your voice and say words like

-I'm tired of this shit or why don't you just leave me alone or it's my money, I worked for it just like you or sometimes worse.

-I didn't tell you to get married and have nine kids that you could barely take care of, living like a squatter and don't own nothing—

Some words should never be allowed to come into existence at least not from your own child. A phrase that can kill more times than a machine gun because it rings in the night and the day or whenever there is a quiet moment or when people are telling family stories of events that changed everything.

When

daddy went after Dix it brought the house down. The neighbors next door and across the street came running when Fray ran out of the house screaming for help, for someone to stop her husband from killing their son. Dix fought as hard he could but none of them, the whole family, could not stop his father's determination to give him the beating of his life.

-so I'm just a squatter to you huh. and your momma says I'm mean. boy that's the meanest thing you could've ever said to me and the last thing you gone ever say-

If

Dixan had not taught the boy how to fight so well, it would have been much worse but it was bad enough. The neighbors finally got them separated

and nobody escaped without busted lips and noses. even the baby girl had received a lick or two so enraged had Mr. Evening become.

-that's a mean man Ms. Evening, mean-

Dix

moved down to his father's brother's house a few blocks away.

-Dix why did you say that to your father. you know ain't no man gone take that. a squatter? what was you thinking-

-Oma don't start please. he was getting on me about coming up short with my part of the money for the house, you know bills and stuff. I don't know, it was the way he was asking me questions like he was playing with me, like I was a little kid he had caught in a lie-

-well, weren't you lying-

-yeah, but not like he was saying-

-yeah but you were lying weren't you? you didn't tell him about that expensive coat you put in the layaway did you?

-are you crazy man he would kill me if he knew that-

-looks like he almost did...is that coat worth all this. I pay rent too. com'n now I love you and all that but Dix we got to live in a real world. We are black and we belong to a race of black people and we don't have a whole lot. Most of our parents been through hell and back. Some of them are half crazy just trying to feed us and raise us. I'm the baby girl and my sisters is grown and they still have to help out. My momma just like your momma, she ain't never worked a day in her life. I ain't talking about farm work where they grew up I'm talking about city life. I do day work up in the heights for them white folks and I make my weekly contribution-

-what you saying Oma you don't want the coat?

-I'm saying anything that cause too much trouble is it worth it? but mister man it ain't for me to instruct you. you the man. if we gone be together then you need to make decisions like a man not like a boy-

Women.

Even

when they young they say things that can get a man all turned around, sometimes to the left sometimes to the right but don't seem to make much difference once they put that one word in that gets him to thinking. So Dix, mister man, had some serious thinking to do after talking to Oma. The one thing he realized is words can make a powerful impression and his mouth was still sore. Even Oma's sweet kisses couldn't soothe away the pain.

-Dix your father has been drinking a lot since you been gone. the other night they brought him home from the corner bar and for the first time in over a year he missed a day of work. yes it's that serious. he swore to me that drunk or sober he would never hit anybody again. he cried like a baby when he realized he had struck baby T when she tried to stop him. The whole family is just sick. we need you home Dix, my legs are aching and my back is sore. no no not the fight . . . from worry. you don't understand son the whole house seems so empty without you in it. I think your father understands now that he can't treat you like a kid anymore, teasing you about lying to him. you weren't lying to him were you son? you were spending the money on that girl you like so much. I told him that a boy nowadays got to have a little change in his pockets to take a girl to the movies and a soda or a dance.

-yes, momma things are different now. you remember what you told me about me how things were when you and dad were young growing up in that little town, what was it Oglethorpe, yeah. I can't imagine anything like that. miles and miles of farms, hayrides and buckboard wagons, dirt roads.

-yes but you live in a different world Dix and that's what your father and I wanted for you and your brothers and sisters. Won't you come home now son I miss you-

-well, momma yes but there is something I need to tell you first-

-tell me later. I got your favorite cooking in the oven, roast chicken, dumplings, and apple pie and bring your uncle More when you come.

As

you've probably figured out we're getting down to the end of this story. Dix still faced how he had lied, well not really lied but left out what was really in lay away

He had even lied to Oma as well his daddy. One day while he was making a delivery of Carson's suit, the man that owned the bar on sixty fifth, one of his friends asked him to drop off a package since he was going that way. When he dropped off the suit he told the man behind the bar that he also had a package, the man nodded his head and gave him five dollars.

-what's this for-

-the package-

Dix saw his friend a couple days later.

-what was in that bag-

-did you get paid? ok, that's all you need to know-

-what you got me mixed up in Bedny. you and your boys always doing something crooked-

-well, if you thought that why you take the package. stay out my face sucker-

Dix

punched Bedny several times before Bedny went down.

-you just like your daddy. damn man, you Evenings are some crazy folks-

-I tell you what next time you want me to deliver something you better make sure it's clean-

-aw come on man, I'm just trying to make a dollar like everybody else, ask your daddy-

-what you mean ask my daddy?

-why you think I chose you? wasn't no accident. what, you think your daddy and your uncle's choir boys? man you better wake up-

-you better get the hell outta here-

Dix

always thought of his father one way. I'm sure like many of us, we just can't imagine our parents as anything but parents: momma and daddy. but in truth, they were young people too, making mistakes or doing things to survive. Everybody does it, it's just that when you're a kid that world just doesn't exist for you. Dix was growing up in America where men become men in time.

-you just become what you become-

He

didn't go out and kill no beast or hang bear claws around his neck or repeat after me's, survive in the wilderness for forty days and forty nights but he knew now more certainly than ever that he was becoming a man. his bones in his body felt different and his mind took on tangents a few months ago he could not imagine. The red coat was like an engine on a track carrying him down the road of life.

If

I were going to continue this story I would tell you in detail about how happy everybody was when Dix returned home. I would go much further into how he became a delivery man of extra packages and how he ran into his Uncle Hank and his daddy at Carson's making deliveries when they were supposed to be getting drunk at the corner bar. I would probably tell you about the famous crap game where Dix won over five hundred dollars of which he gave one hundred to his father. That was done on the road of the secret passageway men come to and exchange information they keep to themselves and away from the family.

-son, I'mmo tell you this, don't think for one minute that women don't communicate with one another in secret. they got they own road they travel on where they meet and exchange information and do things away from menfolk. that's the way life is. if grown folks didn't have these roads there would be killings everyday-

As

you might imagine the Christmas the Evenings celebrated that year was the best one the family could remember. Fray had tried on a black coat like the red one and Dix had put that in the layaway along with the one he got for Oma. Oma met the family at Christmas dinner although everybody already knew who she was. The shoes that Dix had put in layaway were for his daddy who hadn't bought a pair of new dress shoes in five years. Black Stetsons with the white stitching and a black Stetson hat. Dix had taken his winnings from the crap game and "other business" and had bought himself a car, which of course became the family car.

-Son I must tell you I'm very proud of you and I will tell you this day that in my eyes and in the eyes of the whole family you have become a man. And who is this pretty young thang you got sitting on your right come to bless our dinner table-

-This here...

-I can speak for myself, I am Oma Grance-

-Oma, you know I often see your mother at the fish market-

-you know my mother Mrs. Evening?

-Oh, yes, I know your mother. We've walked to the same fish market for many years. The next time you come over we'll spend some time together talking and I'll show you a few of my favorite recipes that always work-

The

next year America entered the war and drafted many of its finest young men to join in.

-Oma I'm not asking you to wait. Nobody knows how this thing is going to turn out but if you tell me with all your heart that you'll wait for me then you'll make me a prisoner of your love. I'll be like a man serving a sentence behind iron bars where no bullet or bomb can penetrate and when my time is done I'll come home and take care of you the rest of our lives-

-I'm not waiting for you unless you're my husband and I become your prisoner handcuffed with a ring on my finger and shackled by a chain of love from my heart to yours-

If

I weren't trying to end this story I could tell you about their marriage when he can home from boot camp and the three years they were separated while he was away at war. I could tell you about the baby boy born nine months after they were married and the five children they had after he came home from the war. The houses they owned and everything else that makes a complete life. But if I told you all that I would have to write a book or two so, let's just end this now or you can just continue the story in your own words in your own imagination.

Thanks Dix for telling me this story to pass on to all the children of the Evening family

your baby brother Light Evening

THE LEADER

The

men sat in studied silence in a certain room beyond reach of the stage. The short but taxing walk to this building gathered them in more than a resting place but a virtual hideout. Their backs and arms weary from all the pulling and touching. The inner self of men spilled like water onto the hard concrete. It was spring but inside the heart of the people it was winter. They had shown a willingness not only to listen they had shown by their applause that they now believed. Love showed itself to be a driving energy.

The hour of departure drew near.

-how shall we leave?

Only

four of the five heads moved as eight eyes scanned each other in the room. The question seemed unusually loud. A state of confusion existed among the group and Ovey noticed his comrade's vacant stares. A coldness pricking around the perimeter of his heart that he had first felt when the men returned. The final round of scouting completed.

-is there something I should know?-

Again

the eyes began searching one another only this time the probe was deeper and more prolonged. The brows creeping higher into furrows of skin wrinkling on their foreheads.

-what the hell's going on. we've just listened to the most inspiring reception given the man and the four of you sit there looking one from another. I heard everything on the speaker box after his speech ended. did something happen on the way back here. Anvil? Reed? Herol, you always got so much to say. what about you Aelous-

The

large single light in the room reflected off their brown foreheads. The room smelled of nervous sweat. Ovey paced the floor in front of the men, their silence ominous. Herol shiftred guiltily. Anvil's eyes bucked more than once.

-he will be here in less than five minutes and this is the way were going to greet him. man this room is like a tomb. what happened after he left the podium. somebody attack him. has he been hurt?-

Without warning Reed slumped in his chair and fell to the floor, gasping for air.

-tell him, tell him . . . for god's sake somebody tell him-

-it's not going to be bad as you might think– Anvil began.

-it will move the people– Aelous completed.

-Anvil, Aelous what are you talking about. spit it out in plain English. what will move the people.

No

one ever thought a black man could reach this far this soon but it happened. That was four years ago when he became governor then the run for the presidency. It was three days before the votes would be cast over the video. The President of the America's, the most powerful office on the planet. Population one point three billion with a GNP of thirty trillion dollars. A standing army of nearly ten million and a land mass from the northern to the southern Arctic. The results broadcast on three hundred hi-def bands with a voting population of over six hundred million. Muto had taken the Union of the America's by storm. His good showing at last week's debate in the Union of Panama United along with a highly received speech delivered in Haiti had pushed him into the front of the remaining ten candidates vying for the job. The global response of the four billion that had watched the speech was in the sixty percentile the highest anybody had received in over fifteen years. His campaign based on the slogan "remember the shortened people." All those millions who were suffering because so many companies were offloading work to the Moon and Mars abandoning the homeland for the treasures of the new frontiers. Husband and wives separated by long journeys to these off worlds, especially Mars.

-tell me, what is being done for the people?

-Muto will be shot-

-shot! shoot the man who will become the first black president of the United Union of The America's??? Ovey was at the top of his voice.

-shot. wounded not killed-

-are all of you crazy? you know I won't go along with this-

-it's too late. grab him, hold him Herol-

-I told you this skinny little punk would never go along with this Anvil. get up Reed, you're almost as useless as he is-

-well, maybe he'll understand this we got too much money tied up in this deal-

Ovey was punched into quick submission. Herol kicked him viciously.

-stop it you bloodthirsty bastards. Muto is the target. Reed can you at least watch him. it's time for us to go. this will all be over in the next few minutes.-

-Reed, Muto is our friend how could you be a part of this?

-it's out of my control now. the committee planned this. they always plan these kinds of things. nobody can stop it-

-who's going to do this?

-somebody they chose. any second now, any second– Reed said staring at his watch.

The

noise of the crowd reached them as expected. Suddenly a terrible chorus of awful screams drowned out the cheers.

-it's done-

-I didn't hear a shot Reed? Ovey expressed, his voice full of grief.

-it's done. too much crowd noise to hear a gun shot-

A

minute later the door flew open. It was Herol. His face looked like it had been hit by a hurricane; the sounds from his mouth a human maelstrom colliding against the walls of the concrete complex.

-Muto made an unexpected move toward the crowd. He was stabbed twice by some lady wielding an ice pick seven inches long. She stabbed him in the eye. my god man in the eye with an ice pick. he died on the spot-

No

one else said an audible word as the rest of the conspirators arrived grieving uncontrollably. Out of this came a sinister laugh erupting from the broken soul of Ovey. The foreheads of the conspirators took the blows of the sinister laughter, evil in its intent. Deep waves of ridicule in contrast to the tricks of fate chasing the plotters from the war room of planning.

Ovey chased them with his sinister laughter until

they disappeared from sight. He pounded them into madness as they ran amuck into the surging crowd looking for escape from the scene of murder.

-god forgive you I never will. you hear me I never will.

Never-

MANY FACES

The

year was 1908 and my Uncle Leroy was making his way home after twenty-five years panning for gold and silver in the Rockies of California and Nevada. He was now fifty or more, he never would say exactly.

1928.

Twenty years ago seemed just like yesterday. We were heading across Death Valley towards New Mexico to my parents' house. I was out of school for the summer. Uncle Leroy, my dad's brother, decided to ride back with me. We were a good hundred miles into the desert when he asked me to stop. I did and he just sat there looking around like he was trying to remember something he had forgotten. The only thing I noticed was this mountain in the distance. Funny I hadn't noticed it before. It was a dark reddish color on the bottom and blue on top with a patch of snow for a cap. Uncle Leroy had his hand on his chin looking behind us at a grove of wild trees with little berries hanging from them. I could hear these birds whistling. The desert was hot, wavy lines rising up from the sand diving into the sunlight.

A

few moments later he asked me if I was still writing stories and I said yes. He looked me right in the eye then and said, "I'm going to tell you something boy, something I ain't never told nobody. I want you to listen good cause you only gonna hear it once. Write down every word just like you hear it, understand?"

I shook my head.

This is the story he told me that day.

-The morning I left them hills after all those years, twenty-five years of hard digging, I finally hit a vein. Popped it good. See them mountains over there, the blue top one, that's the girl that gave me my golden baby. Yes, sir. I loaded my three mules with as much as they could hold and lit out. I made five trips like that over the years. The last trip I packed and left without once looking back. I had found this perfect spot to bury my treasure. Back then there were no roads like this and it took several days to cross this desert. A man had to watch out for bandits or running short on water. I carried six large canteens. Rode mostly at night. Now for some reason this trip seemed to be taking a long time, at the time I thought that was kinda strange. I couldn't get moving so I traveled during the day but then the sun wore me out. I decided to rest so I pitched me a little lean-to to keep the sun off me. I slept the rest of that day, early afternoon until the moon came up. I started out soon wanting to unload my gold and get back home. I rode that night and most of the next day, not hurrying but moving along. It was well into the next night when I decided to stop. I was worn out. I had been traveling now for five days. By now I would have had my gold buried and be on my way home. Something wasn't right but it wasn't until the next day that I found out what it was.

"It

must have been a little past sunrise. I woke with a start. Something spooked me. I reached for my rifle but there was nothing in sight. The sun popped up over this dune like it was staring at me. I felt real uneasy although I couldn't see anything but it was there, that feeling. I decided it was time to get moving. I was packing up my gear when all of a sudden I heard it, this whooshing sound. It was a sandstorm coming fast from the South. Boy, I'm telling you I ain't never seen no storm arrive so fast. It was on me before I knew it. I lost sight of my horse and pack mules. I covered my face and laid down praying I wouldn't be buried alive. Then I heard another noise, a deep rumbling, shaking the ground. My skin was vibrating as fast as that sand was spinning. I looked into the storm and coming right at me was this big white circle. It stopped a short distance from me and everything just got real quiet and still. Then I saw two huge red horns on a fiery blue face come prancing out of that white circle.

"Riding on the back of this giant beast was the biggest Indian I had ever seen coming straight at me. I wanted to run so bad but my legs wouldn't work. I stood there froze to that spot."

"I must be dreaming, I said out loud. I'd never heard nothing like this. Never imagined this was possible. The giant buffalo breathed loudly, snorted and came to a stop not more than ten feet from me. The Indian leaped from the blue beast back and walked toward me, stopping not more than three feet away. He was real all right and my body was shaking so hard my neck hurt. When he spoke, his voice seemed to come not from him but from everything around us so that I felt his voice even in back of me.

"I am Chief Many Faces. You have interrupted the sleep of my people and walked on sacred ground. I am the guardian of this land since before the white man had his first council. Since before the white

man ever came to this land. Upon you and others that have violated this sacred ground is a curse. Your final day will be here among the bones of my people."

"Ya should'a seen it. All around me bones started rising out of the sand. I heard voices of the dead speak. I saw visions of another time. Long before the white man came. I saw wars and famine and chiefs and great ships and an opening between this world and the next and an older world so long ago it was incomprehensible. I closed my eyes and my mind went blank.

I

woke up just like I did before. I woke up in a start only this time I had no feeling that something was wrong. I thought for a moment that maybe I had had a really scary dream or something until I saw one big hoof print left in the sand. It wasn't until I got back home that I became aware ten days had passed not the usual five or six. I thought I must have a fever and stayed in the bed for the next week. The thought of that Indian and buffalo filling my head. Time passed and I sort of relaxed and came back to myself, eventually pushing the whole thing way back in my head. Anyhow I ain't never told nobody this story for fear somebody would think I was just a little touched. Anyhow, it don't matter now anyway.

I

must have had the most incredible look on my face by the way my Uncle looked at me.

"It's time for me to go and just as quick as you can get the hell out of here. Take this note it'll tell you where the gold is buried. Have a good life."

Uncle Leroy got out of the jeep, smiled at me and headed out into the desert. I called to him but he kept walking. I tried to start the jeep but it was dead. I jumped down from the jeep and started to run after my uncle. He turned to me and his voice drifted eerily to me: *do not follow me, remember the curse.*

Suddenly

a sandstorm appeared from the South swallowing

Uncle Leroy. It disappeared in a matter of seconds. I found his watch and a piece of desert glass that I swore had an image of his face shining in it. I packed up and left the desert shaking like a leaf for many days.

THE BOXES

Smoke

rushed for the street. The owner followed with a handful of little boxes. He then rushed again into the smoke. His hands were hot as he emerged with several more boxes tossing them into the street. A slight wind changed the smoke to flames. Two men smoking cigarettes approached. Sally, the owner of the bakery shop across the street, looked out her window. The two men entered her shop butting their cigarettes on the brick front. They each bought a dozen donuts. They watched the man fighting the small bonfire in the street.

"Why is that man burning wood in the middle of the street?"

"Will Gay? hope he don't burn down the whole neighborhood," Sally smirked. "I don't know what's come over that boy. Been doing that now for almost a year."

"Well, why haven't you folks done something about

it. Man like that ain't safe to have around if he burning wood in the middle of the street like that."

"We was going to have a meeting but the sheriff's horse died suddenly and –"

"Horse? a horse stopped a meeting?"

"that horse was nearly forty years old!"

"A forty-year-old horse?"

"Listen at yourself, Jorus, let's just get these donuts and get out of here. Thank you m'am and goodbye. Come on, Jorus. A forty-year-old horse," the man said chuckling.

"This is an odd part of town Melvin," Jorus said as they closed the door behind them. Shaking their heads and firing another cigarette as Will Gay put out the last of the burning boxes.

Every

Tuesday for the past year Will Gay could be discovered rushing from this shop with burning embers. His first performances were met with curiosity. But after several months the novelty began to wear off and dissension began to wag its tail. The last meeting was canceled but a new one had been set two weeks from the day the horse died. That was two months ago. It seems the sheriff had taken ill and some members were out of town or something, summer vacations.

"Well, I never heard of such delays," Sally spoke to Emma in the back of her wedding dress shop.

"You know some of the other merchants don't want to do this," Emma expressed.

"And why not," Sally protested. "seems to me we got to do something; don't you agree?" Emma's silence told the story.

"You're just afraid to speak up because of that expensive dress he bought from you. How much was it, over two thousand dollars I heard? Is that true?"

The phone rang before Emma could answer.

"Oh, let me get that– hello, yes, yes, ok fifteen minutes. Yes, and thank you."

Facing Sally, Emma said with her eyes slightly narrowed, "I'm so sorry Sally but I got to run and do some measurements, you understand we'll talk later." She reached for her favorite yellow sweater and headed for the door.

Outside Sally said under her breath, "just a bunch of cowards" and went back to her store.

Will Gay

stared vacantly at the last pieces of charred wood. For exactly one year he had been trying to bring into reality a vision, a concept. It started with his mother telling him that all men have a purpose in life and that he must find his. Will Gay's father had been a cabinet maker and it was from him that Will learned the secrets of the trade. His father loved what he did. When he wasn't making cabinets or small tables and signature desks he could be found sitting outside the back door whittling small wooden toys and human figures. Most of these he gave away, especially around Christmas. Will was eleven when his father died. His father's helper, a Mr. Elroy, took over the duties of keeping the shop open. Will went to work in the family business.

After school and on weekends Mr. Elroy showed Will the things he would need to know to make a finished product and the staining process his dad used to make his signature furniture pieces. They worked with no written designs only cut pieces specifically made for whatever style of furniture they were making. The six wood cuts for making a tabletop or the sideboards of the hutch or dresser and the spindled table legs and which glue to use and the right cuts to make for joints and the weight of each desk once it was finished. Will also had to learn pricing and shipping and bookkeeping and what he found most curious of all was how much to pay Mr. Elroy. Only specialty items like beds or sofa frames were crafted based on old designs Will's father kept in a black leather book. Will's mother Gladys had never had anything to do with the business and could only provide meals and common sense things to her fast- growing son.

Will

entered his twenties when his mother passed away after a short illness. A note from Mississippi took Mr. Elroy back home to take care of his ailing sister and spend the last years of his life down by the mighty Mississippi. "Will I still hear the sound of that mighty river echoing in my ears. Fish just a-hopping and the bull frogs singing deep into the night. Sorry to leave like this but ain't much more I can teach you anyway. You got a natural gift for the wood boy, just like yo' daddy."

And with that Mr. Elroy was gone. Will was twenty-two when he left. The little street had grown into a small but stable district of shops and the city Natural Pine had grown. Situated not far from the lake in northern Alabama, south of Chattanooga and Northwest of Dalton it was a perfect little spot for city folks looking to get away for a weekend of unspoiled mountain air and Will's daddy's shop was known to turn out some of the finest handmade furniture in a hundred mile radius.

Now, Will's mother, although not known as a

businesswoman proved to be quite enterprising. Because of her the shop was moved from the shed to its present location, 101 Apple St. She had also saved a lot of the items Benjamin Gay had whittled and painted, selling them as souvenirs. She had almost got a deal with a furniture store in Atlanta to carry the furniture Benjamin made when he suddenly died killing the deal. Gladys's veneer peeled away after he died. She never recovered her vigor. She was now soft flesh after the loss of her man. The melodies of her Caribbean childhood returned and the stiff education she received in England faded. She had always reacted badly to Will's dreaminess and Benjamin's whittling, both of which she sought to reverse. One of the last things she did before passing on was to purchase a large tract of land, almost half of a hill not too far from the Georgia and Tennessee border. It was a forest of trees with two dirt roads and a river nearby.

Will

quickly reaching the age of twenty-five, was now forced to concentrate on work. He knew no other livelihood and found that he was just as good if not better than his father. This was all he knew until two events happened simultaneously. He was nearly thirty and although he had come to enjoy wood working, even taking up his father's habit of whittling he still had not discovered his purpose. His mother had told him he would know it when it comes because it would fill his soul with a much-needed new wind.

The

seedlings of Cedar, Walnut, Poplar and Oak Will had planted ten years ago on the South section of the ten thousand acres of land were growing fast and the natural pine that had been cut away and reseeded showed signs of being another good crop in a few years. A deep valley on the West end had three peaks that looked like feathers so Will called it Three Feathers Valley. It was full of granite and sandstone and shrubs but not many trees. He was standing looking over this area thinking of a way to get something out of it.

The

day he met her she was calling for help. Her voice

carried on the wind and echoed off the edges of the ridges and natural hollows. Will himself had spent hours up here throwing his voice around only to be answered by tourists attracted by the magic of the sounds repeating themselves over and over.

". . . help . . . help . . . help." the plaintive pleas continued bouncing around in the air above his head.

"Where are you . . . where are you . . . where are you." Will called out spinning around.

"by the red rock . . . by the red rock . . . by the red rock . . . "

Familiar

with the area he reached her in a few minutes. The twist in her body at the bottom of the ravine told the whole story.

"Thank god you fell here," Will said without thinking, "this is the only place up here where the mountain echoes. The ground up here would have just swallowed up your voice and no one would have heard you." Will took hold of her soft hands and lifted her up. He lost his ability to speak as she stood up, leaning on him for support. "You're beautiful." he said, again without thinking.

The

mountain very softly repeated his words and that's when Will became aware of his purpose. It slipped right into his soul. The echo, how?

The

lady he was helping became frightened by the confused look on the face of the man that had just told her she was beautiful a second ago and now had the strangest faraway look on anybody's face she had ever seen. "Are you ok, you look . . . what's the matter?"

Will

looked again on the woman's face, staring for at least two or three seconds and at that moment he knew who he was and what he would do. He would marry this woman and he would find out why mountains echo. Maybe he could copy it somehow. The smile returned to his face. "Let's get you to town and all fixed up." He was going to find out how the earth can talk.

Elisha Wish said I do before she knew it.

"That is one strange boy," Sally said. "Goes up in the mountain where he finds this beautiful woman and then they get married as soon her broken arm heals. Her legs still broke though. Even in that wheelchair doesn't she look taller than him? Emma you listening to me?"

"Every word Sally. Could you stand over there you're blocking my light and if I burn this dress with this iron I'mmo have to replace that panel and I don't feel like doing that."

"All you do is work, Emma, don't you ever take a break?"

"I don't have little helpers like you, Sally. I'm not from here. It's just me. No family like you have to help out."

"Where you reckon she from? And how come she was up on that mountain anyway?

"Well, they said her family left her land up there and she had walked on Will's land accidently.

"Who told you that?"

"The preacher. Sally I got to go and deliver this dress."

"How come you don't have your clients come here?" Sally asked looking around the shop on the way out.

"I make more money delivering and then I don't have them in here fussing around asking a lot of questions." Emma flipped the switch turning out the light.

"Hello, Emma. Hello, Sally," Will yelled out from across the street.

"Hello," they said in unison.

Sally said under her breath, "hadn't been speaking."

Emma gave Sally a look of disgust, "you know you really need to stop doing that."

"Doing what," Sally said defensively.

"Talking under your breath, people hear you, you know," and Emma walked away without waiting for a reply.

Sally hurried into her bakery not feeling the least embarrassed. "They can all just go to hell as far as I'm concerned."

Will Gay

in one day had made himself a happy man and for the first time ever he felt complete. And Elisha Wish was beautiful. She was excellent in many ways and dutifully assumed the bookkeeping for Will which she described as atrocious. After a couple of months while she was recovering she got his books straight and after they were married she took on the task of expanding the business. First she convinced Will to hire more workers and after discovering his system of keeping everything in his head she convinced him to write down the instructions for everything that he built, then she took it to a local drafter and had it all placed in a book that his workers could follow. Will however kept the book at the house in a safe and would not allow any copies to be made. But this did make his load lighter now that he had six assistants working for him. A grandson of Mr. Elroy had been brought in and Will made him foreman once he saw how well he worked. For the first time in years Will had time to daydream and so he let his mind go and go.

One

year to the day after he was married, in late Spring, in the month of May near where he found Elisha he was sitting there not thinking of anything particular when he heard three blue jays start to sing. The sound whistled across the valley into the mountain and then came back, echoing. Will's eyes chased the sounds as they traveled back and forth taking in the whole scene. He closed his eyes as he focused more intently seeing in his mind the sound travel over the landscape into the stones and ravines and nooks and crannies, slipping across the brook and disappearing for a couple of seconds only to come racing back, echoing the sound like a recording, a phonograph. Will felt the excitement growing deep in his soul. Every fiber of his being on fire with what he must do. So, engrossed he forgot that he had left the mountain and gone into his shop to build the greatest musical box ever. One that required no moving parts, no mechanism, no levers or pulleys. No timing device or recording skin.

"No," Will said out loud. "I will build a box that can echo on its own."

That

was a year ago and after hundreds of designs and many episodes of him running into the street discarding another burning box of failure he had alienated his neighbors and driven his peace-loving wife into fits of despair.

"Will I'm trying to understand and I have been more than patient, you know that but don't you want to have a family, children to raise?"

"You know I was more than a little disappointed when your brother let it slip that it was not an accident you were on the mountain that day but we're married now."

"Oh, Will, everybody knew what a recluse you were and after I seen you I knew what I wanted. But that fall that broke my leg that was not a part of it. But we already had that argument. This idea of yours, this echo thing, maybe it's just not workable."

"Yes, Lee, but I'm so close I can feel it."

"But that thing is so big it takes up the whole shop, you've had to delay projects. Gary quit a month ago. These men have families." She stopped talking and took Will's hands and put them around her waist. "I want children, Will, while we still young."

"I know but it's the only way to build it, nature is big so it has to be big." Will said taking her arms from him.

"And if it doesn't work will you give it up?"

"You mean stop tr..."

Elisha put her finger over Wills lips.

"Listen Will, I know what this means to you to do something nobody has ever done. We've got land up in the mountains where our wood is brought down to make our furniture. You've got a master cabinet maker, a furniture maker, two apprentices and four trainees ready for the new shop. I've gone over notes your mother left and have contacted three distributors very interested in carrying your products. It's time for us to start a family. We've been married over two years and I can't do it alone. I need your help?"

Will

felt helpless when she talked like that. Elisha weakened him but in his soul he knew he was so close so he said, "I'll make a deal with you..?"

"A deal, are you crazy. Haven't you been listening to me. I don't want a deal I want my husband to make love to me. I want you in bed with me, all of you. Not you and that thing."

"I understand, just hear me out, please. All of my life I have been trying to find happiness. I got lucky because I discovered two beautiful things at the same moment that completely changed my life. The only problem has been I can't give either up. I'm not going to lose you and I can't stop chasing this dream either, not when I'm this close. One more week, no two.."

"Ten days, Will, ten days."

"Ok, ten days and then I'll put it away for a while."

"Awhile? what are you talking about awhile. A month? A season? Christmas?"

"Well, yeah, maybe 'til winter when things are slow."

"And then you'll have me spending cold nights in bed like you did back in January."

"No, no, honey, trust me. It's spring now we got summer then fall and I've got new furniture designs, more modern, up-to-date."

"Ten days Will, that's it."

Today

was going to be the day, Will thought to himself. All

the pictures of the mountain were hung around the shop. Books on radar, sonar whales and bat studies, music books. He had real sand, dirt, stones, shrub trees, water for creeks. He had measured and re-measured each contour, the distance and the height. He had never studied anything so intensely. He had gone up to the college and got books on sound waves and spent time in recording studios, he was so full of information a professor he had talked to for over three hours he admitted that there was nothing he could tell Will that he had not already researched. He had everything done to the micrometer, not being a math student, the ratios were excruciating to his brain and he had even cussed more than once, something he never did.

Will

stood back and looked over what he had created. It was ten feet seven and three-quarter inches high and it was thirty-three feet long made in the shape of a guitar without the neck everything made to scale to duplicate the area where Elisha had fell. It was midnight as he placed the final stone in place at the top of the mountain. The great moment had arrived. He climbed the ten-foot ladder and looked over into what was without doubt a remarkable piece of construction. It looked exactly like the mountain itself and Will smiled to himself and then a brief moment of fear gripped him as the idea of failure approached him like a living being. Then he thought of Elisha and accepted the fact reluctantly that she was right. If this didn't work they would have a family and he would put all his energy into expanding the business. They had already looked at a new building on Staccoto Blvd, a new business zone more accessible to the highway.

"Well, it's now or never," Will said and then let out a loud yell and thought he heard or felt the wind. "What the hell was that?"

Before he could finish the thought his voice came booming back to him toppling him from the ladder. Will landed hard on the concrete floor and broke his ankle. His scream of agony was answered by a scream from the box.

Pain and joy filled him.

Sally heard the commotion and darted across the street as fast as her sixty year old legs could carry her. She came into the work area and came to a halt when she saw the immense structure which in her mind had the appearance of an ark.

"I knew this boy was strange but this takes the cake," she said under her breath. "Will is that you screa..." the words died in her throat as the box answered with the sound of her own voice. It was more than her mind could accept so she just turned around and went back to her store muttering to herself.

Elisha was not certain who called but found out later it was Emma. She also heard the screams of Will but was not as startled as Sally had been and had gotten Will an ambulance marveling at the big box that echoed.

"Will, it truly is amazing," Elisha said feeding Will with a spoon. He had broken his back along with his ankle. "The doctors said you'll be fine in about eight months. What will you do with it, it's so big."

Will

was stuck to the bed looking down at the cast covering his chest and stomach and ankles with three of his toes exposed in the other two in splints.

"You know Lee I've been thinking about that for the last three days and I've come to the conclusion that the box, although unique, has no practical value. It's too big to sell as a toy for children. I got a call from the government but when I gave them the dimensions they said they would call me back. Even my friend at the college said it was quite an accomplishment and they would probably give me some kind of doctorate or something but the thing is so big unless it's sitting in a museum or a big hall there's no way to present it to the public and they wanted me to know if I did it would have to be taken apart in sections. It's too big for the shop. I can't get more than five people in the shop to see it. It's just too big."

"What are you going to do with it Will? I thought you knew what you were going to do with it when you finished it."

"I guess I didn't think about that when I was building it. Looks like I forgot the most important step."

"Yeah, the forgotten step of the buyer."

"Huh?"

"Buyers always know where they want to put things."

DRACONIA

Most

tales begin as murmurings from the dark corners of misty nights told near a heaving fireplace. These stories are whispered from ear to ear with the sounds of thunder and flashes of lightening in the background. Other tales rise from the realms of mystic mysteries ritualized by tribal traditions. But some tales form in the heavens appearing on earth as truth stranger than fiction.

Nature

sacrifices itself daily by consuming itself cunningly designing its limitless vacuole characters with a charm to delight its victims before they are devoured. Other victims are classic battles of speed and strength. This is a tale of family heritage, fantasy and prophecy. Becola Delafel was the mother and the carrier. Draconia Delafel was the ancestral daughter in whose blood flowed a poison that transcended space and time. She had blood in search of a mate.

-It's me-

The voice came out of the darkness. I peered into the shadows aware of her presence.

-What do you want. She dying and I . . . we wanted to spend these last hours in peace-

-She's still my mother-

-And you abandoned her-

-I won't deny that. The chocolate made me sick. Poisoned me against her-

-And what about me. What did I get? He was only nine years old and not one word. Not one. Not a letter. Nothing. And what the hell brought you here tonight? Did you talk to somebody or was it the wicked side of your dormant self alive in her calling out to you-

-I sensed it-

-Been eating chocolate huh-

The two combatants faced each other. She stepped into the little light the opened door let out.

-My god look at you!

The mishappened figure shrunk back into the dark. His words pushing her backwards.

-It is what happens to those who suffer from this desire-

-But your face. You were so beautiful and now . . . now-

-Now I have the appearance of one of the ancients. My skin is so hard. I stopped combing my hair years ago. My mind locked on missions, coming out of my skull. My pores bled . . . the sun drying the blood and . . . and . . . This is the mark on me. My fingers tearing at the ground to get the roots of trees. The berries and grapes I mashed to make the wine my body craves to wash out the scent of chocolate. None of the rivers I bathed in could wash away the colors my skin absorbed. I am the clay and life is the paintbrush. I have become this as the others before me-

-Draconia, I am sorry for what has happened to you. We got a letter from the hospital after you left. After your attack. It is a mitosis you suffer from but unlike any the doctors had ever seen. They sent letters here for years. They wanted to examine you-

Over their heads a loud tapping began. Thump thump thump. Then again, more insistent. Thump thump thump.

Lines looked up in the sky as if that was where the sound came from. The storm clouds were speeding by making the moon appear to be sailing. Stars out of reach seemed to be happy to be beyond the reach of the storms below twinkling like white Christmas lights. Lines considered the right and the wrong of this, after all it was her mother not his. None of them would ever see each other again after this. Death was certain and since he had no idea where Draconia had been he had no idea how far she might have traveled.

-It's your mother-

He said more as a statement than as a resolution.

Stepping aside he let the twisted figure in. Looking at her in the light and remembering her great beauty, her sexiness when they were young and the joy they had experienced was a whole different lifetime away. He looked at her without emotion as if they had both died and come upon one another midway through the journey of another life. He knew her not at all.

Draconia stared into the eyes of Lines hoping there was still something there but what she saw was not even revulsion. It was worse. Love still flowed in her veins. His hands looked as loving as ever and she fondly thought of the many nights of foot massages and backrubs and fingers that brought her delights to make you sweat. Her breath came out.

-What did you say? are you alright? Are you weakened? Sit, sit over there– Lines could smell the strong odor of her being outdoors. Stale and dry decaying skin.

All this sincerity Draconia noticed was said without touching her only a gesture and finger pointing, directing her where she could rest. The poison she carried forced a tear of regret from her eye. A guilt not her own, an inheritance she never prayed for.

-Did you ever think how I felt. Uncontrollable urges. The gathering, the searching. I never believed in curses or magic or any of that stuff. If my mother had known she was a carrier or my father do you think they would have joined to make a monster like this. Lines can't you even look at me? Am I so disgusting now?

-None of us blames you. You don't know the places I went looking for you. I even went to your ancestral home in South America. I could not find you so I came home and raised our son. I could not believe that chocolate, I just could not believe that-

-What time is it?

-Five-thirty-four-

-Five-thirty-four?

-The same time our son was born. Five-thirty-four

in the morning. Why didn't you tell me Draconia? Why didn't you say something?

-How is little Ben?-

-Little Ben is forty-seven. Drives the Ox Bow bus line. No wife. No children. Half crazy and still angry at both of us. He blames me for keeping it secret as long as I did. And you, you know why he hates you-

Draconia's eyes wobbled in her head. The dark mist around her mind a never ending maze of cobwebs that drove her into fits of fury from time to time. Suddenly she stood up and walked in a circle, then another. Around the couch then the chairs, three of them. She was counting. She stopped at eleven and went back to her original seat.

-Are you ok?

-Yeah, I just get nervous, you know-

-1980- Lines said.

-1980? Draconia said, coming out of her nervous

fit.

-I ran into my cousin Mountain, a couple of months ago. You remember him don't you? Funny I should have seen him. A friend of mine had just opened his new doctor's office and he came strolling in. His eyes got big when he saw me but I calmed him down easy enough-

-How is he?-

-Well, unlike some of the others he ain't completely crazy and he ain't dead but he did tell me he was stuck in 1980-

-He was the one that raped that dyke bitch- Draconia said remembering more of the past than she wanted to.

-Yeah, said she was just a waif. He was high on drugs as usual, they both were and he just went in her without asking. It damned near killed both of you when the oozing started-

-Well, that dirty bitch shouldn't have raped me while I was in that coma. The maintenance man caught her licking me and when he tried to get her

to stop she told him she couldn't. They had to call security to get that dyke off me. She got a hold of that chocolate and went crazy. Told them she smelled me from the hall. Had a hyperactive nose or something. Damn if she had never done that who knows. Draconia's mind drifted back to the times when she became the monster she is now.

–The doctors said she triggered something while I was in that gestation period. Said they had never seen anything like it. The sweet smell of a brown liquid oozing out of my pussy. They had to wear masks. That's why they wouldn't let you or anybody else anywhere near me. Had me all isolated away from everyone-

-Mitosis– Lines said.

-Mitosis? Draconia repeated.

-Your grandmother's mother knew. How old was she?

-A hundred and fifteen-

-I still remember the day she flew in from Bahia. The doctors thought we was crazy too, remember!

Lines took a seat across from Draconia his eyes bright for the first time in years.

—No, you don't remember your ass was out, gone, but you had this smile on your face and your eyes were wide open. Little Ben had turned your stomach into a small hill and your hair was growing almost a quarter inch every five days. Your great grandmother brought some herbs she had got from the ancestors of the original people. Amazon elixir. She told us the story that had been told to her, an old legend. A woman had strayed on her mate, a mad woman that lived on chocolate. Legend had it that she was infected with some kind of worm as a child, went into a deep sleep and when she woke she had changed. The medicine man said he saw her in a vision ravaging men except the one man she chose to be her mate. Any woman whose blood was poisoned with the worm would suffer this fate but as long as she never strayed on her chosen mate no one else would suffer. According to the legend her mate's brother had always wanted her and killed his brother and took the woman by force to be his mate. Soon after he went mad and died but because she laid with another man the worm poisoned her blood and drove her to eat chocolate and make a drink of berries and grapes and eat the roots of trees and shrubs. Her great beauty attracted the men who became her victims and she infected them with her brown liquid. The worms passed during sex poison to men and it would drive them mad before they died a horrible death– Lines paused for a moment as if to catch his breath.

She became a dark figure. Some of the legends say that her hard skin is what started the original people to work in clay. One legend said that she lived a thousand years. Some said that when she went to sleep she would go into a cave and sleep fifty years her body encased in a shell of hard skin covered with hair. When she awakened she would ravage the tribe stealing the men in the early morning hours with her beauty and the sweet smell of chocolate. One night with her and within months the men would go mad and eventually die.

The medicine men pointed to the heavens, to the serpent in the sky and called her Dracoda—the bad one comes to earth.

While Lines was speaking Draconia was undergoing imperceptible changes as the urges of Dracoda began to stir deep within her. Lines was her mate, the man that was chosen by destiny to save her. Lines didn't notice how much more erect she sat or the slow change in the appearance of her hair. Draconia was on the move preparing to engage another victim. Despite her love for Lines the Dracoda was stronger and she hadn't had any satisfaction in over a month. It was time to feed the worms beginning to swarm in Draconia's womb. It was the swarming that caused the smell of chocolate and the fluid to seep past the lips of her vulva. Lines was talking up a storm, his hands turning his words into images as if he were directing people on a stage.

-None of the original people ever ate anything sweet until they became adults. Any child caught eating cocoa was killed immediately as it was feared that the Dracoda worm would be awakened by the eating of the cocoa bean that would ferment and become chocolate. Your great grandmother said that it had been over five hundred years since the last time a woman had become the Dracoda but the legend was still alive. They said her beauty was so great and the smell of her chocolate so hypnotic that men and weak women would become her victims. Even knowing what would happen they would come. They found the Dracoda deep in a cave encased in her clay like a cocoon pod and to make certain she wasn't just sleeping they hacked her into fourteen pieces and removed her sexual organs and burned them in separate fires-

-But why did this happen to me? Draconia said her voice clearer and younger as the Dracoda in her continued to slowly come to life. Lines still hadn't noticed the changes occurring in front of him. Perhaps it was the room with its one lamp on a table by the door. The seats they occupied on the opposite side of the room by the main hall where the steps led to the upstairs. Or maybe it was the hypnotic fragrance of chocolate permeating the air ever so slightly dulling the senses of its victim like the bite of a spider, only this venom took to the airwaves to snare its prey.

-The doctors said it was a genetic defect that causes a reformation of membranes. The Dracoda worm is passed down through the female generation after generation until the right combination of genes, blood type, and chromosomes comes together and bingo– expressing his frustration Lines stood up turning his back to Draconia.

-Hell, they don't know maybe it was the moon, you know like a werewolf or something. The shit is fucking crazy, scientists don't know everything. They been studying your blood for forty-seven years and they don't know any more now than they did then-

-Do you believe in those legends? Draconia's voice had now definitely taken on a younger quality. She sounded more alive not the raspy disfigured hag that knocked on the door some thirty minutes ago. So, she lowered her head so that Lines couldn't see her face as he turned to respond to her question. She pulled the thick shawl she wore around her covering her arms and hands and lowered her body into a hunch.

-Do I believe in them? Look at what happened to you. I lost my brother, my son and you tell me how many other men have come to their end attracted by your chocolate? How many have you pulled down into your world?

-Stop it, Lines. You make me sound like a monster. I am not a bad person, not evil . . . I have a problem but maybe together we can stop this . . . make it go away.

-Draconia it won't work. Remember what you did to us?

-We didn't mean for that to happen but your brother . . . he was weak, the smell of the chocolate it got in him-

-And what got into you, lust? You weren't even infected with this thing then, were you?

-I was– Draconia said her head down and her voice low and away.

-What did you say? Don't whisper, tell me for god's sake, you've kept secrets long enough. You and your mother-

-I knew something was wrong, so did my mother. It was when we were in Panama at the great canal. My father slipped and fell in and my mother jumped in to save him. They both nearly drowned and were saved by some men on a boat that rescued them. While my mother was recovering I was taken to my aunt's house. I was three or four. I found some chocolate one night and ate it. I didn't wake up until a week later. My skin was covered with ash and my hair had grown nearly two inches. My mother's and aunt's faces looked awful; it scared me that's why I remember it.

-She is just like great grandma's sister, the one that died in the jungle killed by the tigers-

-The old people said he came because of her smell but then they chased the family away afraid that one of the other children might be a bad one waiting to hunt them one day-

-The legend said that one day Dracoda would return-

-And so from that day on I was always watched. When I was nine I was taken to my ancestral home by the Amazon River near Bahia up in the hills. I was taken to a shaman who examined me in a cave. He looked in my places-

-Places? What do you mean places?-Lines was standing over Draconia wondering why she no longer looked at him. He couldn't see her face but he noticed her voice was different. She sounded younger but he thought maybe because she was sitting she had rested and had regained some of her strength but he thought maybe he should keep an eye on her. He had no idea how much he could trust her. He had no idea what to look for and did not know what he should do to defend himself should she attack him in some fashion.

-The shaman was in my holes, any place where a worm can enter but especially in my sexual places. If there was a serpent there sleeping they wanted to try to awaken it. If it was there I would have been hacked to death and burned. He pushed on my navel with a wooden staff and then then jabbed at my places until I bled. My grandmother took me to a cave and gave me a broth and my grandmother Towak oiled my skin. I went down in a deep sleep and when I woke up I was back in my rooms by myself and I could hear voices arguing.

-You must take her away-

-Are the people coming?

-They are coming. If you do not go . . . if they find her they will kill her-

-Is she the one-?

-The shaman wasn't certain she is so young but she has the ash and her hair did grow and she is beautiful, unbelievably beautiful-

-What about the smell. Does she have the smell of chocolate?-

-She has a fragrance but she is so young it is like a wisp but in later years it will flower especially under the full moon when it is close to the earth, the harvest moon. The moon and women, especially this woman, will reach its heights during these times until she reaches the age of nineteen. Hurry get her to America. Never let her eat chocolate and when she gets eighteen you must tell her the legend. She can only have one man and that man is to be her mate, he must take her first. Only she will know him. It is the lust of another man that brings Dracoda to life, if that happens you must kill her. If she escapes and lives until the next full moon nothing of man can kill her except her mate and that is only if she chooses.-

Lines stared at the top of her head with a certain feeling of dread creeping along the edges of his thoughts and in the pit of his stomach. He felt his heartbeat increase its tempo and a cold sweat leaked across his forehead. His voice was cold with the temperature of an animal that suddenly realized he was being led into a trap.

-You never told me that. Your mother never told me that. What the hell kind of crazy shit is that. You come here in the dark of morning somehow sensing that your mother is dying. I have the brutal memory of you lying with my brother producing a son that for nine years I thought was mine. You're scaring me you know that-

-I'm not trying to scare you Lines but I'm tired. I'm

tired of the killing and the monster inside me, swallowing me up, torturing me with all the devouring. Don't you love me at all, don't you want me . . . want to help me-

. . . thump thump thump . . .

Lines nearly jumped out of his skin. The thumping seemed to thunder over their heads from upstairs. Draconia looked up and Lines saw now why she had kept her head down. The disfigured face of Draconia was gone and in its place was the great beauty he remembered she was.

A weak voice called from upstairs—Lines, Lines, do you hear me . . . Lines-

The following moment of silence passed slowly. Lines watched Draconia rise up from the seat she seemed resigned to and display an exquisite nubile body. The sight took Lines' breath away. His eyes couldn't believe what he was seeing. This was not possible his mind was thinking but his body was saying something entirely different as he felt himself falling under the power of the Dracoda.

Lines heard the dragging sound of the body upstairs. Draconia moved closer to him, aware of the power of the smell of chocolate as it coiled in the air taking him captive.

Now the body upstairs had dragged itself into the hall. The voice of death coming from it as it dragged itself calling out –Lines . . . Lines- so full of hopelessness and agony.

Time seemed to stand still for Lines as his eyes took in the beautiful woman in front of him. Even her feet were beautiful as she slid closer to him.

-Lines . . . Lines

The next moment the body upstairs took on human form and spoke in a tone of great alarm- Lines, Draconia is she here? I smell chocolate. Tell me she is not here. Lines why don't you answer me? Help me. . . . please. Draconia if you're here please don't do this . . . please-

The body started dragging itself again.

Lines was stuck between worlds. The past of Draconia now enticing him and the voice of her mother pleading for life even as she was dying. Draconia now was only focused on her mission. She was the legend that she never wanted to be. A horror show. A serial killer spraying her victim with sexual acid filled with worms that would destroy their victims from the inside, some quickly, others more slowly if they didn't get a full measure but die they would in a mad world filled with worms feeding on their brains. She was now fully transformed and Lines unlike most victims got the chance to witness the flower at its peak. The years of separation seemed to fly away as she got closer. Lines container of sex began to fill with a lust he did not know was there. They both heard the body as it dragged itself onto the steps but still out of sight of them. They could hear the labored breathing between the agonizing calls for Lines, 'help me please' and the thump of the body as it landed hard on the next step falling not walking or crawling.

Draconia's lips were full of flavor but foul for what was intended. Her eyes sang a song of the end is near. Yet, Lines felt himself yielding willingly conflicting with what in his mind could not be right. Draconia stood now not more than three feet in front of Lines. Draconia's voice was smoky, heavy with lust as the moisture in her churned. Naked and warm she removed Lines shirt and placed her mouth on his lips with horror playing an image in his mind while his hands undid his belt buckle. His old heart of love broke ground, coming clear as he reached for her moved by his desire to taste her. Lines lost his bearing and went wild in Draconia's jungle swinging in with no thought of anything especially impending death . . . he did not stop.

How can the moon fight against the light of the coming sun? One rules while the other sleeps but Draconia would finish this dance before the light of day.

Draconia whispered into the ears of Lines

–you must make love to me and as soon as we are finished you must kill me while I am in my most weakened state. You are my chosen mate and only you can end this. Lines listen to me . . . please, you must kill me. If you do not I will devour you whole so that I may live on. I need your flesh to complete myself . . . Lines do you hear me-?

Lines nodded yes as he fought with his mind but his body failed him and no number of sermons could save him from the desire to mate, to consummate that which was his destiny. It was what he was born to do. Just as Draconia was selected so also was he genetically matched as her twin without the worms but the missing component to complete her.

The body of Becola had now drug itself down the stairs where she could see the two naked figures in the living room. The smell of chocolate so strong she coughed as she spit up phlegm, gagging on dying breaths. She would have no memory of the terror in her eyes and would never again ask for help her body folding in on itself as death took her.

Neither Draconia nor Lines had any thoughts of Becola the body on the steps. The ceremony of Dracoda had begun its dance.

-This knife must be plunged into my places before I

can transform. Lines take this knife you will have this one chance, do not hesitate or we will both be lost-

Lines took the knife that she had been holding behind her back.

-There are poisons on this knife designed to kill me do not miss-

Lines could no longer resist the smell of the chocolate and began by tasting her breast. It was alcohol passing into his mind, heady with a rush pushing him forward to open her up. They attacked one another with ferociousness, like two wild animals. They found each other by the mouth looping into deep and foreboding body gyrations. The end would be near for one of them as they fought with the passion of life and death, pleasure and pain, they thrust back and forth.

Draconia!

Lines!

Draconia!

Lines!

And they exploded together with a yell and a sloppy kiss.

-Now Lines, drive the knife deep into my places. Do it now before I transform, hurry, save me -

Lines found himself looking into her beautiful face and his life passed in front of him. One day he was a child, then a man in love with a woman who was more beautiful than he could imagine. Now she was asking him to end her life with a knife plunged deep into the place where only seconds before he had fulfilled his lust in a liquid paradise of chocolate honey. Lines had never been a direct person, thoughtful rather than an action hero. It was for this reason that life had always selected men like him as a mate for the Dracoda, men who would hesitate in that moment when hesitation, even if it cost them their own lives it was exactly what they would do. It is the dance of life how each has its own natural defense against the enemies that attack it.

-Fool you have waited too long-

Lines was jerked back to the present by the powerful hand of Draconia. Lines made a vain attempt switching the knife to his other hand and plunging the knife in the direction of her places as he was on his knees between her legs. He missed and struck her thigh, blood oozed out. Draconia locked her legs around his neck as he struck again striking her near her places the knife going in halfway up the blade. Draconia yelled out in pain and squeezed even harder as she transformed rapidly into the tragic figure with clay like skin and haggard face and hair. Lines tried to scream but unintelligible words stuck in his breaking neck. An animal caught in a trap he knew he would not escape. Draconia laid him over on his side as the oozing from her turned into chocolate acid which she spread over Lines. She began to devour him feeding the parasitic worms of Dracoda.

-You should not have hesitated Lines. You should not have hesitated-

When she was finished she never gave a single thought to the final episode of her mother, Becola, the body on the steps. Lines was just debris. She didn't close the door when she left. The moon had given way to the sun but she didn't care. It had been a good night and nobody paid any attention to the old hag shuffling down the street eating chocolate and humming, smiling like a two-toothed kid.

...have I been this way before, it sure seems like it...

About the Author

Master Poet Hzal Anubewei is his name of enlightenment. His birth name is Anthony Fudge. He was born in Cleveland, Ohio and currently resides in Lithonia, GA. He is a published poet, author, and playwright. He has appeared on radio and TV and was a writer in residence at Albany State in Albany, Ga. He recently completed a mystery novel *Studney and Kilapot: The Two Moons* will be published summer of 2020 along with a book of poetry *AMA*. He is nearing completion of the second book *Second Schemes* in the series called Schemes. His style of writing has been compared to *Rimbaud* in a 2009 review by Jendi Reiter of Winning Writers.

He

was one of the founders of Black Ascenscions Magazine of Tri C Metro, The Oar; a theatrical company, and won an award from the Cleveland Area Arts Council and was published in their first Anthology. He has read with many national poets among them Russell Atkins, Norman Jordan,

Gwendolyn Brooks, Larry Neal, Amira Baraka, Nikki Giovanni, and Carolyn Rogers to name a few. As Robert Flemming, noted New York author once noted, *"Fudge has to write, as necessary as an arm or a leg."* Art Nixon referred to him as "the poets poet". Owen Dodson after reading his poetry book The Cry of Beauty (1976) called him a 'word magician'.

Hzal

is also the author of several plays: Migration 1973, They Sing Songs About This 1977; and recently an Africanized tale of Cinderella called Fanta and Rooli performed at The Clarkston Community Center 2018. Other plays he has written include Heimalacay (a blues opera), Arolynn, Diary of the Genius of Love, and Promises Kept.

A

project closest to his heart is the establishment of Oetryhouse, a physical structure for poets where they can meet, exchange ideas, house video and audio recordings, present poetry, hang framed poems, and entertain the public. For too many years poets have no place that they call home. Contact Hzal at: oetryhouse@gmail.com

Hzal Anubewei Fudge

OETRYHOUSE

WHERE WRITERS TAKE CARE OF THE WORD

www.ingramcontent.com/pod-product-compliance
Lightning Source LLC
Chambersburg PA
CBHW020734250626
47155CB00003B/748